The New Zealand Book of the Beach 2

Also by Graeme Lay

NOVELS AND SHORT STORY COLLECTIONS
The Mentor
The Fools on the Hill
Temptation Island
Dear Mr Cairney
Motu Tapu: Stories of the South Pacific
The Town on the Edge of the World
Alice & Luigi

YOUNG ADULT NOVELS AND CHILDREN'S FICTION
The Wave Rider
Leaving One Foot Island
Return to One Foot Island
The Pearl of One Foot Island
Nanny Potaka's Birthday Treat

NON-FICTION
In Search of Paradise – Artists and Writers in the colonial South Pacific

TRAVEL
Passages: Journeys in Polynesia
Pacific New Zealand
The Cook Islands (with Ewan Smith)
New Zealand – A Visual Celebration (with Gareth Eyres)
Samoa (with Evotia Tamua)
Feasts & Festivals (with Glenn Jowitt)
The Globetrotter Guide to New Zealand
Are We There Yet? A Kiwi Kid's Holiday Exploring Guide
The Best of Auckland
The Miss Tutti Frutti Contest – Travel Tales of the South Pacific
New Zealand – the Magnificent Journey (with Gareth Eyres)
Inside the Cannibal Pot

EDITOR
Metro Fiction
100 New Zealand Short Short Stories
Another 100 Short Short Stories
The Third Century
Boys' Own Stories
50 Short Short Stories by Young New Zealanders
An Affair of the Heart: A Celebration of Frank Sargeson's Centenary
(with Stephen Stratford)
Golden Weather: North Shore Writers Past & Present
(with Jack Ross)
Home: New Short Short Stories by New Zealand Writers
(with Stephen Stratford)
The New Zealand Book of the Beach

The New Zealand Book of the Beach 2

Edited by Graeme Lay

David Ling Publishing Limited
PO Box 34601, Birkenhead
Auckland 0746, New Zealand
www.davidling.co.nz

ISBN 978-1-877378-24-9

First Published 2008

Selection and Introduction © Graeme Lay 2008

Front cover: 'Sunbather' by Tony Ogle, 2007. Reproduced by
permission of the artist.

Typeset by Express Communications Limited
Printed in China

Contents

Introduction

Readers and reviewers responded positively to the first *New Zealand Book of the Beach*, whose stories reflected the affinity of New Zealanders with their country's long, lovely coastline. Showing a keen awareness of the role that beach and sea provide in our national consciousness, the first book's contributors depicted many aspects of New Zealand coastal culture, in stories drawn from the era of Katherine Mansfield through to the present day.

Submissions were invited for this, the second *New Zealand Book of the Beach*, early in the New Year. Other contributions were garnered from previously published collections. The editor's brief to prospective contributors, although clear, was also challenging: the stories had to reflect the beach's emotional power as well as its physical presence, they had to show its role as an intensifier of human feelings, a beach setting had to be central to the story's characters and events. In response to the invitation for submissions to *The New Zealand Book of the Beach 2*, stories flowed in like a rising tide, from all over the country and from overseas.

In an era of rapid social and physical change, the beach remains an abiding and constant presence in the lives of nearly all New Zealanders. During high summer – the period from Christmas through to February – they flock to their beaches, which become teeming recreational and social centres. Camping, baching, swimming, surfing, sailing, fishing, hiking, games: these are the physical activities our beaches provide the setting for during the summer months, playgrounds for old and young.

But the beach is also the setting for much deeper human interaction, providing everything from emotional balm to aphrodisiac. For nearly all people, a beach's appeal is primordial. With its unique propensity for heightening human emotions, the beach is common ground for the beginning of a relationship, as well as for the ending of those built on sand. Family holidays beside the sea provide indelible memories for almost all New Zealanders, while the increasing popularity of beach weddings is yet another indication of the emotional significance which we attach to our beaches. In these ways nostalgia and certain beaches become inextricably entwined in our memories.

The twenty-two chosen stories reflect much of the allure, beauty and potential dangers of beach and sea. The beach as a place of sanctuary, and as the setting for sexual temptation, are recurring themes in this collection, while as other stories show, at the beach pleasure can quickly turn to peril. The collection includes childhood stories and adolescence stories, comic and tragic stories, Polynesian and Pakeha stories, stories of beaches past and beaches present, stories of love, hope and despair, stories of escape, stories which reflect the attitudes of indigenous New Zealanders to the beach and some which are based on the reactions of visitors to our shores.

Beach and sea are not just an integral part of the New Zealander's birthright, they also provide the settings for memorable human experiences and hence the raw material for notable fiction. *The New Zealand Book of the Beach 2* continues the celebration of the unique role the beach plays in New Zealand's physical, social and literary consciousness.

— Graeme Lay

A Summer Thing

Alice Glenday

The man who married my mother had a friend who had a bach at the beach. Each year, generally late in the summer holidays, we were allowed to rent it for a week, or sometimes two. The difference seemed to be due to the friend's not keeping a record of how many other friends he had that year. He was a schoolteacher, like my stepfather Clarrie who said he didn't blame him for not keeping records out of school.

The bach was one in a small East Coast settlement on a bluff above a sandy beach. For some reason, possibly the tortuous gravel road that led to it, this perfect place wasn't popular. That suited, or alternatively didn't suit, each of us according to our need at the time. When Mother and Clarrie first went there they were on their honeymoon, and I'm sure the lack of people was no hardship. Now, seven years later, despite the troop of us that accompanied them, it's possible that they craved some stimulating company.

Or perhaps I'm transferring to them my own sixteen-year-old yearning. For what, I'm not sure. Possibly a soul-mate. Or more likely, remembering the previous summer, something more down to earth.

Yet one of my joys in being at the beach was in the solitude it offered. I found pure pleasure in leaping down the sandhills and skimming across the early morning beach that was all mine except for the seagulls. I would send them screaming and soaring as I waded into the foamy shallows, jumped up and down with shock, and plunged into the waves. I felt a kind of purified virtue as I looked back at the still-abed bach on its rise.

It was too small for us, of course. Part of any problem that arose was due to living at such close quarters. There was a tent that went with the place, and Kate and Bill slept in it whenever possible. When it rained they kipped down in the living-room. Neither set-up was considered satisfactory, and Kate was heard to comment that celibacy was said to be good for the soul. Bill said, 'Fine. So what's new?' And then there was silence.

Later that day Mother said, with contrived lightness, 'You know, Clarrie and I have always wanted to sleep outdoors in the tent. Would you mind if we changed places tonight?'

'Yes, I would,' Kate said. 'So forget it.'

We might have if Clarrie's mother hadn't heard Kate too. Mrs Claridge, or Rosa as we'd been invited to call her, had started coming with us a couple of years ago, after her husband died. Now she was taking up a room that wasn't rightly hers. Clarrie, whom she called John, said not to be silly Mother.

My mother, whom Rosa called Margaret though she was known as Maggie, said, 'Please don't say that, Rosa. You have every right, and we love having you.'

I can't believe Mother did, especially when Rosa called her Linda, the name of Clarrie's dead first wife.

Clarrie, renowned for his relaxed good nature, said sternly, 'This is Maggie, Mother,' as if introducing them. 'My wife.'

'I'm so sorry, John,' Rosa said. 'You'll have to forgive an old woman.'

Rosa was a tall gaunt woman with blondish-grey hair that reached to her waist when she let it out of its bun on the nape of her neck. 'I was once an ash blonde,' she said sadly, and Clarrie, more gallant on that occasion, said she still was. She was said to be of the old school, and I conjured up dim dormitories and straggly crocodiles of hatted girls. She veered from being imperious to pathetic, and for some strange reason I liked her.

Betsy, my half-sister, did too, which was perhaps even more surprising as Rosa didn't dote on her as grandmothers are supposed to do. She called her by her proper name, Elizabeth, and seemed to expect her to behave accordingly. Betsy tried, and became rather quaint, but of course couldn't live up to such expectations. She spent much of her time at Rosa's side, which must have been tiresome for Rosa but was fine for me as I had to share a room with Betsy at the bach.

I was fond of Betsy although she was now nearly six. She had been lovely as a baby, when she'd stayed nicely in place. I didn't like her so well once she started going into my bedroom at home and trying out my lipsticks and things. When I complained Mother said, 'I agree with what you say, Emma, if not with the way you say it. I make no excuses for Betsy, except to say that she is not yet tall enough to reach a doorknob.'

What Mother was saying, in her delicate way, was that it was my fault as usual.

No, that's not fair. Mother, that bright spirit, deserves better.

She deserved better than having to put up with such a disparate group of us at the beach, where things blew up more quickly and dramatically than anywhere else.

It is a theory of mine that everything is more so at the beach. The sun shines brighter, the rain falls heavier on the spirit. People become more basic, and almost believe it when they say they're going to give away the rat race and become beachcombers.

Not long after our arrival the previous summer, Kate trapped me in a hollow among the dunes and proceeded to have a little talk with me. Why she felt constrained to periodically do so when I had a perfectly good mother I don't know. Perhaps, being older and married, she felt better able to communicate with me. She wasn't. I inwardly fumed at her schoolteacherly lectures, which had become more technical since she and Bill had taken up extramural studies to compensate for their not having a baby. I bore with her because of the things that she presumably knew that I didn't.

'Are you aware,' she said, 'that a holiday by the sea can, like an ocean cruise, arouse one's libido?'

'One's what?'

'Sexual emotions. Lust, in other words.'

I hardly knew, at fifteen, what that meant either. What I did know was that Kate had never been on an ocean cruise.

'You're crazy,' I said. 'I don't even like boys.'

That wasn't quite true. I liked Jim, who lived down our street and sometimes got off his bike to walk home from school with me. And certainly I liked Bill, and had grown to like Clarrie. But because of that happening with Uncle Adam, I didn't like men. What it came down to was that I didn't like to be touched. By anyone.

So what was I doing, that summer I was fifteen, in the sand dunes with a boy who was holidaying at another bach?

Not, as it turned out, very much. But the inexplicable thing is that I was, on some level of my being, willing.

I'd been aware of this boy, gangly and rather gawky, on the beach the day I arrived. We pretended not to notice each other but we both showed off in the sea. Before long he joined me there and we splashed and leapt and dived. Or as the boy, Leighton, said, dove. He was a visiting American and, I was to learn, fast. Certainly he lost little time in chasing me towards the sandhills where, out of breath from all the nervous exertion, I allowed myself to be caught and kissed.

It was my first taste of kissing, and it left a lot to be desired. It progressed during that week from ill-aimed slobbers that sent me scrambling to escape, to drawn-out scorchers that set my passion on fire.

Yet I didn't really like it. And I hated it when he put his tongue in my mouth. It made me gag. I bore with it for the sake of my lust.

For all Kate's warning I would probably have gone the whole way if it hadn't been for my bathing suit. To ring the changes I'd unearthed an old one of Kate's, a shiny blue satin one with a zip up the back. It was so tight that Leighton wasn't able to get at me, and when he slid down the shoulder straps I prudishly hauled them back up. But on our last day I didn't put up my usual fight against his trying to take my bathing suit off. I even tried to help with the zip, but neither of us could budge it.

'It's full of sand,' Leighton said. 'Can't we peel if off without undoing it?'

'No,' I said, my ardour gone. 'I'd never get it back on.'

'Then hold it for me.' He grabbed my hand and held it against an agitated protuberance I'd been theoretically prepared for but wasn't. I drew back. 'I couldn't.'

He turned nasty. 'There's a name for girls like you.'

As I watched him clambering up a sandhill I felt sorry for him, wondered what the name was, and knew I'd never liked him.

Yet I was disappointed when, this year, there was no young man cavorting on the beach. I was going to university in the autumn and needed all the experience I could get.

I sighed and joined in family activities. We walked along the beach, disagreeing on whether it was easier along the shore or higher up on solid sand. Not that it mattered, as we kept our own private pace with the sea. I liked to alternate between splashing along in its ripples, its resounding roar in my ears, and withdrawing to scour the wet sand for shells. Spread out though we were, we'd raise our head to check the others' progress, and if Rosa and Betsy were with us, to wait for them. At some spot, seemingly miles from home because of the tricks the wavery light played at the beach, we'd decide we'd gone far enough.

Those of use still with energy climbed the cliff, here more of a challenge than our home bluff. It was higher and less compacted, and the sand was inclined to slither and start an avalanche. On reaching the top you looked down into a valley of smaller hills and hollows. There was something about those barren dunes, and the blue shadows they cast, that reminded me of the moon. That in turn reminded me of something I couldn't quite place and for some reason, perhaps connected with my father's death, didn't want to.

Looking back towards the sea we'd see Rosa, sometimes alone if we'd hauled Betsy up with us, always sitting facing the sea, head erect, legs straight out in front of her. Once, dropping to the sand beside her, I copied her upright pose and found it excruciating. 'Rosa, how can you bear to sit like that? Don't you find it painful?'

'No more than I'm used to, Emma. I have never found life easy.'

I wanted to tell her that she was purposely making it hard. But I was conscious of Mother's nearness and didn't want to make life harder for her.

Mother tried, in small ways that didn't make her a martyr, to make life pleasant. On our last day at the beach she was up before us to arrange breakfast on the brick terrace. She had covered the garden table with a blue cloth, and had laid at each place a single sprig of something from that unkempt garden: parsley and thyme that someone had once planted, a convolvulus flower, wild honeysuckle, a buttercup, a dandelion head in seed, forget-me-not. When I saw it I wanted to put my arms round her, but couldn't.

Betsy showed enough enthusiasm for both of us. 'We're having breakfast outside,' she trilled at Kate and Bill in their tent.

Bill, the first to emerge, put on a smile and said, 'Great. Just what we need. Fresh air.'

Kate put her head out to say, 'There's no need to be sarky. If you don't like the simple life, take it out on me.'

Bill kept his smile in place as he passed on his way to the shower room. I could have told him Clarrie was in there, but didn't.

Kate came out in her kimono and sat hunched on the steps hugging her arms. 'I suppose I'm last in the queue for the shower.'

When Clarrie came out, he stopped rubbing his hair with a towel and studied the table. 'Whose nice idea was this?'

'Mummy's,' Betsy said. 'Mummy did it.'

He sent Mother a smile. 'I should've known. So that's why you deserted the marriage bed.'

Kate got up and stalked into the house.

'Kate's cross at Bill,' Betsy confided to Clarrie.

'Not to worry,' he said. 'It'll come right.'

'Betsy,' Mother said, 'would you like to go and tell Rosa we're having breakfast out here?'

When she had gone Clarrie said, 'Trouble?'

Mother glanced at me. 'A little.'

Breakfast was not a success. Kate and Bill sat without speaking. Rosa examined the honeysuckle at her place and gave a little shiver.

'Are you cold, Mother?' Clarrie said.

'It's nothing, John. But perhaps you could get me a wrap?'

'Sure thing. Just tell me what a wrap is and I'll get it.'

'A cardigan, John. My white cardigan.'

Betsy eyed her anxiously. 'Rosa's sad today.'

'We're all a little sad,' my mother said. 'The last day is always sad.'

'Rosa's sad for something else,' Betsy said.

'What is it, Rosa?' Mother said. 'Aren't you well?'

'I'm quite well, Margaret. I'm being foolish. It's my wedding anniversary.'

'Is that right, Mother.' Clarrie draped the cardigan round her shoulders.

'Yes, John, it is right. I've been married forty-six years today.'

'Well done,' he nodded. 'Though I'm not sure the last three count as being married.'

'I still consider myself to be. And if you're referring to your father's death, it's closer to four years since he died.'

'Yes, you're right, Mother. And I'm sorry.'

The clatter of cutlery on china was loud in the silence. 'I think we scared the birds away,' I said.

'Oh, I did that some time ago,' Bill said. 'With my little tantrum. Sorry about that.'

'Tantrum?' Clarrie said.

'Forget it,' Kate said.

When she and Mother were doing the dishes, and I was clearing the table, I heard Mother say, 'I couldn't bear it if things went wrong between you and Bill.'

'You might have to,' Kate said.

Why is it that when a day starts wrong for a particular person it keeps throwing hurdles in the victim's way? Why can it not just say, 'There, I've tested you Kate, and though you've not handled it well, you've said to forget it and we'll leave it at that?'

But no. The furies, or whoever is behind such things, pursued Kate all day.

When we were waiting for her to join us at lunch, at the blue-covered table that Betsy and I had given a second chance and decorated with sea shells instead of vegetation, Kate came marching from the house and plopped into place.

'Who is it,' she demanded, 'that keeps putting the toilet roll on the wrong way?'

Clarrie exchanged amused glances with Mother. 'Is there a wrong way?' he said.

'Of course there's a wrong way,' Kate said. 'Just as there's a right way.'

'If you say so, Kate,' he said.

'Don't humour me. Let's thrash this thing out, once and for all.'

'Yes, let's,' Bill said. 'Let's have a good thrash.'

'Why?' said Betsy, who didn't understand disharmony.

I put my oar in. 'Leave it, Bill,' I said quietly.

'Oh yes,' Kate said. 'Emma says to leave it. And what Emma says goes.'

'Does it?' I said, genuinely surprised.

'Don't play the innocent,' she said. 'It's probably you that puts them on wrong.'

'If you're still discussing the toilet roll,' Rosa said, knife and fork poised, 'I believe it was I who put on a new one this morning.'

'Well, I'm sorry, Rosa,' Kate said, 'but you put it on wrong.'

'Kate,' Mother said. 'Would you like to set us straight about the right and wrong of toilet rolls?'

'Yes, I would. They should be put on so they unroll from front to back.'

'Why?' Bill said.

'What do you mean why? That's the way we do it at home.'

'Give it a rest, Kate, he said.

Kate did. But lunch wasn't a success either.

Perhaps to counteract it, Clarrie set up a game of cricket on the beach. He made stumps with pieces of driftwood and stuck them into the sand some distance apart. He and Mother picked teams. I was on Mother's with Bill. Clarrie had Kate and Betsy. Rosa stood down, but sat on a nearby sandhill and kept score.

None of us was very adept. Clarrie had quite a good eye, as they say, and hit the tennis ball some fine whacks. Bill was better at bowling, and I was glad not to be on the receiving end of his overarm deliveries. He modified them for Betsy and really just rolled the ball to her. But instead of being grateful she demanded a proper throw, which of course she missed and it hit the stumps. She was offered another go but shook her head and trudged off, dragging the bat.

Kate was next. She wrapped her hands around the handle, took up a stance, and faced up to Bill. He sent down a fairly brisk ball, Kate swung, connected, and started to run to the other end. But when she saw Bill scoop up the ball she turned and got back before it hit the stumps. 'Ha,' she said to Bill.

This time he sent her a really fast one. Kate hit it squarely and the ball soared skywards. As it came down over the sandhill Rosa stood, put up an arm, and against all the odds caught and held the ball in one hand.

There were cheers and cries of 'Well held', and 'Good for Rosa', and much laughter. Bill ran over and hugged Rosa and kissed her cheek. She put a hand to her cheek and looked coyly pleased and we all laughed again.

No, not all. Throughout it all Kate glowered, and stayed put at the stumps.

'Out,' Bill called as he came back with the ball. 'Out for a duck.'

'I'm not. Rosa's not even playing. How can I be out?'

'Out.' Bill shied the ball at the stumps. 'Out again.' He waved her off.

Kate threw down the bat and stomped up the hill to the bach.

Clarrie tried to keep the game going but it was over. He drew out the stumps and made a formality of offering each of us one of the driftwood sticks. Bill, standing apart, grinned and said, 'No thanks. I'm trying to give them up.' He went striding up the hill.

'Why is Kate always cross?' Betsy asked me.

'I don't know.' If it was connected with not having a baby, it seemed to me counter-productive. 'Come on, let's see if we can find some special shells to take home.'

Mother and Clarrie had gone with Rosa to the bach. Bill came jogging across the beach, dropped his towel and went plunging into the sea.

'Is Bill cross too?' Betsy said.

'No. He's sad,' I said, convinced I could pick up his vibes.

'Why?'

Betsy sometimes said that automatically and didn't demand an answer. We watched Bill head out to sea, change his mind, and come more slowly back.

'Let's go and meet him,' I said.

Betsy couldn't swim, and when we waded far enough I hoisted her on to my back. She clung there, arms hugging my neck, as I played with the waves, leaping as they reached us, ducking as they left us in a trough. Bill wallowed towards us, showing no sign that he knew we were there until, nearly colliding with us, he stopped, tipped his head backwards in the water, and came upright with his hair slicked back. 'Well, look who's here,' he said.

'Emmy,' Betsy said, 'And me.'

'I thought it was.' He met my eyes. 'Do you want me to take over?'

'I wouldn't mind. It's a bit throttling.'

He went one better and put her up on his shoulders. Betsy clutched his forehead and fixed her face in that pinched smile that meant she was trying not to cry. I thought fast and said, 'I know what Betsy would like. To ride in to shore on your back.'

I'm not sure that she did, or that it was easy on Bill to do the last lap on hands and knees. I found it hard enough in the tug of the undertow to edge alongside and support her. When we reached the frothy sand, Bill folded forward like a camel onto his stomach. I flopped down beside him. Betsy got off his back and lay beside me. After a moment she said, 'I think I'll go and see Mummy now.'

I raised my head to see her climbing the path to our bach, and again laid my cheek on the wet sand. The ripples that ran rhythmically up to my knees before draining away, and the surge of the sea in my ear, were mesmerising. I felt the sand shifting from under me. A sudden fear that I was sinking, and alone, made me turn my head to Bill.

He was reassuringly there. When I lowered my head we lay facing each other. He reached out a hand and, lifting a strand of wet hair from my eye, let his hand rest on the side of my head. And then, although I'm sure I made no movement, the distance between our faces dissolved and our lips met. It was a kiss so right in every way, from its beginning to its lingering end, that we might have rehearsed it.

We hadn't. And we didn't repeat it. We drew back, looked at each other, and stood up. Without a word we walked side-by-side back to the bach.

I never knew if Kate saw us. Or whether she was the one who could pick up vibrations. I only know that as we neared the bach she came out of the tent and, striking a stance, said, 'I'm going home, Bill. Now. You can come or stay. It's over to you.'

Bill stood looking at her across the tall shimmering grass. 'I'll come,' he said, and went to her.

One Summer

Adrienne M. Frater

'How much further?' I peel my legs from the seat. 'Why can't I have a turn in the back?'

The Hillman Minx is so packed with camping gear, Dad's removed the back seat and my brother, five years older, is snuggled between sleeping bags, pillows and rugs. Even his breathing makes me mad. 'We'll stop at Kaikohe for petrol,' says Dad, 'and I'll buy ice-blocks.'

'Going to see the tame dolphin?' asks the man pumping petrol. My tongue chases a drip down my arm.

'What tame dolphin?' Mum's ice-block matches the orange flowers on her dress.

'It's been hanging around Opononi. Likes to follow the fishing boats in.'

'Is a dolphin the same as a shark?' I ask, when I've licked my last lick.

'Dumbcluck,' says my brother.

'Explain to her David,' Mum says. 'You forget your sister's only nine.'

'A shark's a fish and a dolphin's a mammal,' David says in the know-it-all voice that I hate. 'That means they come up to the surface to breathe.'

'And they don't eat you?' I ask, with my first shiver in three days. It's been hot for the three days we've been travelling. I knew Opononi was a long way from Wanganui, but not this far. It was Dad's friend Ed, who'd chosen the camping spot. Uncle Ed, who's not my real uncle, is rich. He owns a huge caravan, while we own a second-hand tent. He drives a car with silver fins and this summer he's bringing his new girlfriend. Each time I ask about her, Mum's lips shrink.

We leave the tarseal and turn onto gravel. Dad winds up his window and I stare at blackberry farms and what David calls mangroves. No sand. No sea. No tame dolphin. Just Mum, Dad, David and me.

'Wake-up,' says Dad and he shakes me.

'Are we there?'

He laughs. 'You've had a good old snore. We've even pitched the tent.'

'But you said I could help. You said I could hold the poles while you bang in the pegs.' Large hands enclose my bunched fists as he hoists me onto his back. Although I'm too big for piggybacks I say nothing, for I can smell salt and hear sea. It's so dark, I have to guess how far away the sea is, but as I lie on my camp stretcher, it sounds close enough to touch.

A snorting sound wakes me. I leave the green glow of the tent and head for the beach. A bank, a road, a strip of grass, then sand and the sea. No cars, no people, just the beach and me. I make the first footprints on sand that is golden and across the harbour, fat sandhills sit like loaves of bread.

I hear the sound again, then see the fin. I try to remember what David said about sharks, but all I remember is sharp teeth and a fin. My feet shuffle backwards and when the shark comes to the top, I freeze.

'Want to scratch Opo's back?' says a woman.

'It's not a shark,' I say in wonder.

The woman laughs and when Opo swims closer, she scratches her back with an oar. The dolphin looks friendly, but I tell the woman I'll scratch Opo's back another day.

My mother's wearing a white dress with purple flowers. My mother's not a mother who wears shorts or sundresses that let your back burn. As she scrambles eggs, sweat moons under her arms. 'I saw Opo,' I tell her, with my mouth full of toast. 'She smiled at me,' I say, staring David out.

David dunks dishes into a bowl of soapy water and after drying each, I stack them in the carton we store under Dad's stretcher. Mum, Dad and I each have a camp stretcher, while David sleeps on a lilo. The lilo was his Christmas present and is green. He swims on it all day, but doesn't see Opo.

'When's Uncle Ed coming?' I ask Dad, as we fish from the wharf. Dad squats to put on new bait. I lie on my tummy, watching the sea move between the planks of hot wood. When a tug jerks my line, I catch a sprat on each hook.

'He should arrive some time this afternoon, but his van's already here. A truck towed it up yesterday.'

Grasping each fish round its belly, I tear it from the hook. When I tell Dad I want to see the van, he says it will be time enough when Ed and Valda arrive.

Valda's a name I've not heard before, and as I drop sprats into the bucket, I roll it round with my tongue. 'What's she like?'

'You'll have to wait and see.'

While Dad's giving our sprats to a man launching his boat from the beach, I pester Mum to go swimming. 'Wait a mo.' She wipes her hands on her apron. 'I'll come down and watch you.'

'But it's perfectly safe. Heaps of kids are swimming by themselves.' It's no use – she even pins my pony tail to the top of my head and makes me wear a bathing cap, then standing ankle-deep in water with my towel draped over her arm, her eyes bore holes in my back.

I shiver, but keep walking – past my knees, past the top of my togs, up to my waist, then sucking in a huge breath, push off. The shiver doesn't last, for the water soon warms. 'Catch,' calls a girl, whose name is Janice and we toss a beach ball back and forth and when a dark shape rises and balancing the ball on its nose, tosses it, Janice laughs and I scream. 'It's just Opo,' she says and the three of us play until Opo swims off.

'You've had too much sun,' Mum says after lunch. 'You need to lie down.' I heavy breathe until I hear her soft snore, then swinging my legs from the stretcher, tip-toe outside. I'm sitting on the bank when I hear the loud toot. Uncle Ed's car, silver fins blazing, scatters gravel as it stops. Sliding onto the road, I wave my hands in the direction of the camp gate. Dad arrives next, which is a good thing, as I don't know where the van's parked.

I run along behind, up… up…to the very top terrace, where the beach looks far, far away. Puffing, I straighten my shorts, check my blouse buttons are buttoned and watch Valda's legs emerge. Long, slim legs wearing silver sandals and red toenails, swing out one at a time. 'Hi, you must be Megan.' Long, slim arms wearing gold bangles and red fingernails, stretch like a lazy cat.

I must have forgotten to breathe for a time, for the breath I breathe out goes on forever. Valda moves in flashes and flickers and it's kinda like being at the flicks. A white dress. A silver belt. Painted eyebrows. Raspberry lips. Buttercup hair. When her hand touches mine, I jump. 'You must come and visit,' she says. 'And do bring your mother.'

By the time Mum wakes I've had another swim and this time almost touched Opo.

'I told you not to swim on your own,' Mum says with a snap.

'It's okay, Dad was there and Uncle Ed and Valda have arrived.' The sky shifts and the cloud that blankets the sun, stays a while. The quiver in my tummy stays a while too.

That night we play Ludo and when I tell Mum that Dad's going fishing with Janice's Dad and her uncle has a piano accordion and they're having a New Year's party and we've all been invited and Valda's asked us to visit, Mum gets up and makes cocoa. It's only when David runs inside to grab a fistful of Kiwi crisps, that the frost leaves the air. By then Dad's told Mum she's not to be rude, besides he knows she's dying to see inside the van. 'Greedy guts,' I tell David, my tongue lingering on the last chocolate chip.

'Are you coming?' Mum asks next morning, after swim number three. She makes me wear a dress and tries to tie a ribbon round my ponytail. 'Mum,' I tell her, 'we're at the beach!'

'Hi, you must be Beryl.' When Valda holds out her hand and Mum has to shake it, Mum's lips force a smile. Valda's lips, which are orange today, smile too. 'Come and look round,' she says, 'then I'll make some tea.'

There's a double bed in the far room. It has a pink candlewick bedspread and the bathroom has a toilet, basin and shower. I look at everything closely, while Mum looks at the wall. Next is the kitchen, where everything matches. 'We plan to eat at the hotel.' Valda plugs in the jug. 'But we'll breakfast in here.' She takes out two cups, saucers and plates, each rimmed with gold. 'Do you like lemonade?' she asks and I nod. 'And what about chocolate fingers?' I nod again. Although dozens of questions dance in my head, my voice has slipped down my throat.

We sit in the small living room and Mum tells Valda about Opo. 'How interesting,' Valda says as she pours tea. Tracing the swirls on the carpet with my toe, I'm surprised to hear Mum talking about Opo and am surprised to hear her talking in a voice I don't know. 'I have a daughter your age,' Valda says, slipping a cigarette into a cigarette holder.

'Do you?' Unsure whether I'm more surprised that Valda has a daughter or by the cigarette holder, my words pop out like corks.

As we leave, Valda asks Mum if she can treat me at the tearooms and I tug at Mum's skirt. I know she wants to say 'no', wants to slap Valda and never see her again, but in that same strange voice she says, 'how kind.'

The next morning Dad's already gone fishing when I wake. 'Where've they gone?' I ask.

'Over the bar,' says David, stacking Weetbix onto his plate.

'What's a bar?'

'Where the harbour meets the sea,' he says with his mouth full. 'It gets mighty rough there at times.'

I ask Janice about the bar as we swim. Opo's off with the fishing boats, so we're duck-diving for stones. 'Mum's not happy about it,' she says, when she next comes up for air. 'Dad says he only goes over the bar when it's calm, but Mum says the bar's a brute and what if the weather changes. Janice is a much better duck-diver than I am, but then she'll be ten in March, while my birthday's not 'til August.

After lunch Opononi fills with cars. The day before quite a few people came to see Opo, but today there are heaps more, so when she appears, we toss balls and beer bottles so we can show off her tricks. It's fun at first, but soon there are so many sightseers, there's no room to fish from the wharf and then the store runs out of ice-blocks.

Later, Valda calls by the tent. She's wearing a sundress the colour of butter and her arms are tanned. Even though Mum reckons her tan comes from a bottle, I think she looks great. 'Ready for your treat?' Valda asks. Mum's lips have shrunk again and her breath gives a little snort each time the hairbrush snags my hair.

'Go wash your face,' she says, and only then can I leave.

The tearooms look straight down on the beach. Heads bob in the water and yet more sightseers line the wharf. My ice-cream soda has a fat straw and a long, silver spoon and I want it to last forever. 'Alex learns ballet,' Valda says, showing me a photo of her daughter. Alex wears a tutu and has flowers in her hair.

'I wish I learned ballet,' I say and as we talk and I sip my soda, a warm feeling spreads through my tummy. But when I stare at my empty glass, my tummy quivers again.

'She's buttering her up.' Mum tosses another snapper fillet into the pan. 'I don't like it, Laurie. Don't like it one bit.' Dad clears his throat and after I've dealt out the knives and forks, I pick at a new scab on my knee.

'It's New Year's Eve tomorrow,' says Dad. 'We're going fishing on the tide.'

I wake next morning to Dad clumping round the tent. 'Are you going over the bar?' I whisper.

'Go back to sleep.'

'Is Uncle Ed going?'

'Not today.' He grabs his sandwiches and leaves.

Janice and I spend the morning carting driftwood from the beach. Her tent and her uncles' tents are at the back of the camp and it's there we make the bonfire. One of the uncles offloads hay bales, which we lug into a circle. Mum wanders up to watch for a time, then goes back to the tent to start washing spuds to cook on the fire. Each time she hears a boat, she looks up. Janice's dad's boat arrives back after lunch, along with Opo and a cloud of seagulls. David gets to help gut the snapper, but Dad saves me an eyeball.

'Look,' I say to Janice and squirting out jelly, scoop out the retina and lens.

'Ugh!' she says and doesn't wait to see how beautiful the retina is and how the lens can make the newspaper letters grow big.

Uncle Ed and Valda don't come to the bonfire – they party at the pub instead. But our party's best. Even Mum enjoys it, especially when Janice's uncle plays his accordion and we all sing. I lie back on a hay bale and watch the men drinking beer and the woman drinking shandy and when Dad sings 'The Happiest Night of the Year', I feel proud. There were stars when we lit the fire, but by midnight they've gone. Mum puts me to bed after 'Auld Lang Syne,' but Dad and David get to stay on.

There's no sun on New Year's Day and the sky's more green than grey. 'You're not going fishing again,' groans Mum.

'We promised we'd take Ed.'

'So you'll stay inside the harbour.'

'We'll see.'

The rain starts while we're swimming. Each drop makes a poached egg in the water and small rivers carve tracks in the sand. Opo swims with us for a while then leaves. 'Megan.' Mum's standing on the bank with a towel over her head. 'You'll catch a chill.'

I don't know what a chill is, but as Mum says this, the wind starts to blow and one by one the swimmers leave. 'I don't like it,' Mum says, rubbing me dry. 'I don't like it one bit.'

The tree behind our tent slaps the canvas and the wind starts to sound angry. Dad should be back by now and every few minutes Mum lifts the tent flap and glares at the sea. There are waves in the harbour now and some wear white hats. When Valda bursts in shaking an inside-out umbrella, Mum hands her a towel. 'I'm worried,' Valda says. Her hair hangs in rat-tails and black leaks from her eyes. Mum nods and puts the kettle on. When David arrives and Mum makes tomato sandwiches Valda pretends to eat, but drinks all her tea. As the tree creaks and the harbour, which yesterday was flat and blue, starts to roar, I squeeze my eyes shut.

'It's stopped,' says David, some time later and he bolts from the tent. I listen to Mum and Valda talking in small voices, listen to the gulls meowing and then I leave too.

As the last dark cloud moves away and the wind and waves quieten, I tear down to the wharf. There are no sightseers, just seagulls, Janice and me. 'Did your dad go over the bar?' I ask.

'I think so.' Standing together, but apart, we shuffle our feet.

People gather on the beach. They stand still as statues and not a single person swims. I've not seen Valda on the beach before, but see her now, standing close to Mum. 'Where's Opo?' Janice asks.

'I haven't seen her since this morning.' I swing my legs, 'til my heels thump the edge of the wharf. Seaweed dances and amongst the weed swim sprats. It's weird how one minute everything can be so noisy, then the next, become quiet. Janice says nothing. I say nothing. We wait. We listen. We wait.

'What's that?' Janice asks and I hear a motor. Not a loud motor, but one that coughs between puts. We run to the end of the wharf, wrap our arms round a post and lean out. 'Is it a boat? Is it Dad's boat?'

'Yes. And there's a dark shape in the water.'

Janice breathes, I breathe, and as the boat and the men and the shape come closer, I see Mum and Valda run to the edge of the water. Others run too, but I don't, and leaning out further, we watch Opo lead the boat in.

My Enemy

Tania Hutley

I wish I hadn't come. And why did I bring Justin? It's hardly a good time for playing get to know the parents.

I've spent every Christmas here since I was in the womb, but so what? Everything is different now. Everything that is, except the bach.

They say you should know your enemy. Maybe that's why I've been stalking through each room, running my fingers over surfaces, taking musty books from the bookcase, absorbing that distinctive smell of pages yellowing as their stories slowly age.

Justin and my parents are lobbing platitudes back and forth across an invisible net in the living room. I can't make myself join the game. And that's another thing. Why do I suddenly find it so hard to make small talk? Down here it's a skill that gets constant practice.

Justin's having yet another cup of tea. He hardly drinks the stuff at home, but he's had three cups in the hour since we arrived. He's perched on the most rickety chair at the table; the one that sent Uncle Matt sprawling and has been Supa-glued three times since then. Mum and Dad are on the couch, the one piece of furniture that's younger than I am.

I try to settle, perching at the table next to Justin, and playing with the handle of my own mug of cold brown liquid.

'I heard they'd spotted sharks here,' Justin says.

'Who did?' asks Dad.

'It was on the News.'

'Must have been a slow news day,' scoffs my father. 'Every summer there are sharks off the coast. Don't know what they're making such a fuss for. When was the last time there was an attack in New Zealand?'

'I wouldn't worry about the sharks,' says Mum. 'But we had some jellyfish wash up the other day. They can give you a nasty sting.'

'They're not that bad.' Dad rolls his eyes. 'It's not like we live in Ozzie, is it?'

The curtains in the living room have faded in a rectangle the size of the window, because we always leave them drawn when we're not here. The windows are mottled with years of salt deposits that have drifted across in the wind. When we arrived I ran my finger across one of the opaque glass panels on the door and a residue of gunk is still caked into the lines on my fingertip.

'There was some good surf at the point this morning, Kyra,' says Dad.

I say nothing, and after a few moments he glances away.

'Do you surf, Justin?' asks Mum.

'Um.' He's looking at me, uncertain. 'I've never tried it, but I'd love to learn.'

I get up and take the untasted cup of tea into the kitchen, following the path running through the middle of the door where the patchy varnish has been worn off the wooden floorboards by generations of bare feet coated with sand. I tip the tea into the sink, and turn on the right hand tap. The red symbol has long since fallen off the top of it, but if I didn't already know it was the hot tap I'd be able to tell by the way the water coughs, whines and dribbles its way out, stone cold for ages then suddenly hot enough to burn.

My shell collection has sat on the kitchen windowsill for years, in plain sight, but until now completely ignored. I pick up one of the shells, a flat fan shape covered with dust. It's left a mark on the windowsill. No, not a mark. It's protected the wood, so that the sill around it is bleached and splintered, but there's a small patch of richer colour where the shell was.

I stare at it for ages. Then carefully put the shell back down in the right place, facing the right way.

Maybe I've been too quick to judge. This poor house is not my enemy at all. Its battle scars prove it's a fellow victim, not a malefactor.

Leaving the cup soaking in the sink I drift over to my bedroom. My name is on the door, Kyra, printed onto a rectangular piece of brown plastic. I remember peeling off the backing paper and sticking it on... I must have been seven or eight. The letters have faded, but when I tug at the plastic it's still stuck on so tightly it feels like a permanent part of the door.

Wouldn't it be funny if that cheap, crappy bit of plastic lasted longer than I did? Maybe my name will wear off completely and it will be a blank nameplate. An empty epitaph for a forgotten life.

What an awful thought. Not forgotten, surely? Not for a few years at least. And what more can anyone expect?

Justin says something about me; I hear the sharp 'Ky' sound of my name ring clearly above the muffled volleys of conversation. Whatever he's saying I don't want to hear, so I step inside my room and pull the door shut behind me. My room is so narrow that the set of single wooden bunks take up the entire far wall, with a tiny window allowing a grudging amount of light in above the top bunk. Against the left wall a dressing table takes up a large percentage of the remaining floor space. Although the room might seem uninviting to a stranger, I used to prefer it to my larger, sunnier room at home. When I got old enough to think about why, I figured it was because I admired the way the room contained the precise amount of space required for sleeping, or standing to pull clothes on or off, and not a centimetre more. Something about the purity of its function appealed to me.

Even now, it's the room I find easiest to be in. Probably because it's always so dark in here.

The tiny room seems even smaller with Justin's bags and mine in it. Especially because the dressing table is piled high with nine different wide-brimmed hats. I bought my first only a few weeks ago and now I collect them compulsively. I can hardly go by a hat store anymore; there's one in Kingsland and if I'm going to St Lukes I've started deliberately going the long way, through Sandringham instead. Because if I find myself going past that window with all the hats displayed, I have to stop and go in. I have to buy another hat for my collection.

Justin and I are only here for a few days so I won't get to wear most of them. One has fallen from the top of the teetering stack and is lying upside down on the floor, its fake flower squashed under it. I don't pick it up, even though I've been fussing about the hats all the way here, laying them out carefully in the back of the car before we drove down, making sure they didn't get crushed. When we arrived I carried them in two at a time, each a silent accusation. The one on my head had an extra-large brim, forcing a personal space half a metre wider than normal. Mum and Dad both had to duck under it to hug me.

This is who I've become. Too old for teenage tantrums so I wield hats as weapons.

The blanket on the bottom bunk used to be my favourite; it has a faded print of a surfer riding a giant wave on it. But now there's a rip in the middle that I'm sure wasn't there last time I was here. I bend down to finger the rip, and end up sitting down, stroking the softness of it, feeling the edges of the ragged imperfection.

I've always slept in the bottom bunk, even though down here I'm completely shielded from the window and at night the blackness is thick enough to choke on. So many years of lying, listening to the creak of springs as one of my cousins – usually Diana – rolled over above me. So many years of whispering up at night, of pushing on the wire base if I didn't get an answer, poking her ribs through the thin rubber mattress.

Now it'll be Justin above me. How strange to have him in the room with me, but not be able to reach across and touch him. Funny to whisper up to him, to hear him answer. Like murmuring a prayer into the darkness and having God reply.

I lie down flat on my back, and stare upwards as though he were already above me. Even with the door closed I can hear Mum laughing at something in the other room; a giggle so familiar, like a well-practised piano scale.

Some nights I'd lie on this bunk and Mum would rub an ice-cube on my shoulders. Sometimes I'd lie on my front while she peeled off skin in delicate sheets.

No, stop it Kyra. Those memories are banished.

But I can't help myself; getting off the bed I go into the bathroom, pull open the mirrored cupboard over the hand basin and check the tube of sunscreen. The use-by date takes a while to find, and then to decipher; it's almost worn away. But the year is definitely 06. Which means it expired two years ago.

I throw it into the little plastic bin under the basin where it sinks into the jumble of used toilet rolls. Of course I won't say anything, but maybe later someone will be looking for the tube and might ask what happened to it. I hope they do.

There's another bottle of sunscreen in my bag. Back in my room, I pull it out and put it on the dresser with the hats, creating my own personal shrine.

When I finally emerge, the others are still sitting, talking. I can hardly believe it but, by the way he's sipping, it looks like Justin's accepted yet another hot drink.

The cup Justin's drinking from is printed with 'World's Best Mum' in battered yellow letters. Mum's cup has a picture of a cat on it. Dad's is the biggest and has a cartoon face on the side. In spite of these differences, every cup in the bach matches, one thing marking them out as belonging to a single set: each has an identical chip at exactly the spot where you want to drink from if you're right-handed, as we all are.

'You should replace those old, chipped cups,' I say. 'The chips are breeding grounds for bacteria. And it's not as though they ever get washed properly.'

'Yeah,' Dad agrees. 'We should.'

I shoot him a surprised look as I sit back down at the table next to Justin. Things might have changed a little, after all. Last Christmas when I mentioned something about making the shed more secure so no one could break in and nick my new surf board, he acted like I'd suggested putting in a heli-pad.

'We've got fresh snapper for dinner,' says Mum. 'Brian dropped in with a couple of beauties this morning.'

'He reckons him and Stu were reeling them in faster than they could get the lines out,' says Dad.

'Yum,' says Justin. 'Fresh fish sounds great.'

'When do the hordes arrive?' I ask.

'Uncle Matt and Julie are coming on Wednesday, with Diana. Aunt Sophie and Uncle Ryan come up the next day. Jess isn't coming this year, but William and Peter will be here.'

'Justin and I will leave on Tuesday then.'

'This Tuesday?' Dad sounds shocked.

'You don't want to see your cousins, love?' Mum's voice is gentle.

'No.' They come every year, but this year maybe I could have been consulted. It didn't even occur to Mum and Dad I might have wanted some time by ourselves this Christmas.

So many of my favourite memories had their setting here. Not any more. I had a giant box of photos in my brain labelled 'The Bach', but somehow the seawater seeped in. Now they're ruined fragments that I have no wish to pick out.

'When's the operation?' asks Dad. 'Not until January?'

'Straight after New Year,' I say. 'The third.'

He nods. He already knew when it was before he asked. It's his way of saying I should stay longer. 'You look pale,' he says. Then he flushes, like he's said something wrong. His eyes are confused. I'm sitting across from him in this little room we've sat in every Christmas, year after year, yet he doesn't know where I am or how to reach me.

The riptide of anger that's been dragging me out suddenly lets go. I raise my head and see how far from shore I am, how alone.

Looking Dad in the eye, I manage a smile. The words 'I love you' are somewhere buried inside my tongue, coated with a hard shell of emotion. I'd like to force them out but even the thought threatens to bring tears.

Instead I touch the bandage on my arm. My fingers find the hollow place where flesh should be. Funny, I used to have a bump there and now it's a dip. And after the third it'll be much bigger than a dip. A crater, perhaps.

'Does it itch?' asks Mum. 'You want to change the dressing?'

'No, it's okay.'

'Sure?'

'Yeah.'

She offers an apologetic smile, not to me, but to Justin. 'I don't want to make a fuss.'

Too late for that. Maybe she should have fussed a little more, a little earlier.

'Want to go down the beach?' asks Justin.

'No.'

'Come on, it'll be fun.'

I sigh and drag myself out of the chair. 'Alright. Let me get changed.'

Instead of taking clothes off, I put more on. Another layer of sunscreen first. Then long sleeves, and a long billowy skirt. The hat stays, and I slip on sunglasses. The only exposed parts are hands and feet.

'Shall I go in bare feet?' asks Justin when I come out. He's wearing his normal glasses as he lost his prescription sunnies, no hat, and hasn't reapplied the quick smear of sunscreen I had to remind him to put on this morning.

'What else?'

As we go outside he says, 'I just thought there might be prickles in the grass.'

Like I should worry about him getting a prickle in his foot. I stomp on ahead so he can't see my expression, and climb the dunes. He catches me up when we get down onto the hot sand and grabs my hand, the one not holding my hat on. 'You're acting like it's their fault,' he says.

'I know I am.'

'It isn't.'

'No.'

'Then why are you so mad at them?'

'No reason,' I say. 'There's no reason for it.'

He shakes his head, frowning. I know he's trying to understand.

The wind whips tendrils of my hair under my sunglasses, irritating my eyes. I pull my hand free of Justin's to wipe the strands away. Maybe it looks like I'm wiping tears, because he grabs me in a hug.

'It'll be okay,' he tells me for the zillionth time. 'They caught it in time.'

Without answering, I stare over his shoulder towards the sea. The shadows of birds skim over the sand and vanish into the waves.

That's what I want to do, to disappear into the water like I used to. Back in another life, that is, when the beach wasn't something I was afraid of. I pull from his grip and walk down towards the water.

'Kyra.'

I stop and turn. Justin is down on one knee, an offering held out in front of him, gripped within the thumb and forefinger of both hands.

I take a few steps back to him. 'What is it?'

An answering smile breaks across his lips, ripples up into his eyes. He waits until I'm standing right in front of him before he speaks. 'Kyra, you know that I'll love you forever?'

A group of gulls hover just behind him, gliding motionless on the breeze, waiting to hear my reply.

I pluck the offering from his hands. It's a piece of shell with a finger-sized hole through the middle. I slip it onto the middle finger of my right hand, the fingers on either side splayed out to accommodate its bulk, and pretend to admire it.

There is no forever. Life cuts off on the third; that's as far ahead as I can conceive. Everything after that falls into a black pit of maybe, beyond imagination. There's a chance they'll have caught the cancer before it spread, but when I try to focus on that possibility, it slips away into the depths. This year there is no fourth of January.

It's not until I say the words, 'I love you too,' that I realise it's a lie. Maybe... hopefully I'll be able to love him again once we're away from here and back in the city. When I bend down and kiss him all I can taste and feel is the slimy barrier of sunblock on my lips, but he beams at me like I've sealed a promise.

The seagulls are handfuls of thrown confetti, scattering skywards, blown over the ocean.

When he stands and brushes off the sand, I see that it has tattooed itself onto his knees, so Justin carries the mark of the beach on him. As I do.

Waiariki

Patricia Grace

When we were little boys we often used to go around the beach for kai moana. And when we reached the place where the rocks were we'd always put our kits down on the sand and mimi on them so the shellfish would be plentiful.

Whenever the tides were good we would get our kits and sugar-bags and knives ready, then go up at the back of our place to catch the horses – Blue Pony, Punch, Creamy and Crawford. And people who lived inland would ring and ask us about the tides. 'He aha te tai?' they'd ask over the phone – 'What time's the tide?' and we'd tell them. All morning the phone would ring: 'He aha te tai? He aha te tai?'

And on those days there would be crowds of us going round the beach on horses with our kits and knives, and when we arrived at the place for gathering shellfish we boys would mimi on our kits and sugar-bags then wash them in the salt water, all of us hoping for plenty of kai moana to take home.

We never thought much about the quiet beauty of the place where we lived then. Not in the way I have thought about it since. I have many times wished I could be there, living again in our house overlooking the long curve of beach and the wide expanse of sea. We could climb up through the plantation behind our place to the clearings at the top and look away for miles, and could feel as free as the seagulls that hung in the wind above the water. It was from this hill that I once saw a whale out off the point, sending up plumes of spray as it travelled out to the deep. And on another occasion from the same hill, we watched the American fleet go by, all the ships fully lit, moving quietly past in the dusk.

If we went down the gully and up on the hills at the left we could look back to where our old house had been, then down to the present dwelling with all the flower gardens and trees around it. And below the house by the creek were our big vegetable gardens, which kept us busy all year round. One would have thought that with vegetable gardens to tend, our parents would not have had time for flowers. But flowers, shrubs and trees we had in abundance, and looking down from the hills, or from the beach below, the area round the house was always a mass of colour. But it is now, looking back, that I appreciate this more.

The bird tree was our favourite, with its scarlet flowers like red birds flying. Then there were the hibiscus of many different colours, the coral tree, kaka beak, and many varieties of coloured manuka and broom. And there was a big old rata under which one of our brothers was born, and named Rata for the tree.

In front of the house at the end of the lawn was a bank where scores of coloured cinerarias, black-eyed susans and ice plants grew, and beyond there was the summer house that my father and brothers built before I was born. This was where my father had all his hanging baskets crowded with ferns and flowers.

Where I first left there to go away to school, and when I first realised what other people had in the way of money and possessions, I used to think how poor we children were. I used to think about it and feel ashamed that our patched clothing, much of it army surplus, was the best we had. And felt ashamed that the shoes that had been bought for me for high school were my first and only pair. It wasn't until many years later that I realised we had many of the good things, and all the necessary things of life.

There were ten of us living in the house at the time I remember, but there were older children who had married and gone away. Seventeen children my parents had altogether, though not all lived. I can remember the day my youngest sister and her twin were born. Our mother had been away at one of the top gardens getting puha, and on our way home from school we could see her coming down the track on Crawford. And our father was standing by the gate with his hands on his hips, shaking his head.

'That one riding on a horse,' he was saying. 'That one riding on a horse.'

And Mum got down off the horse when she got home and said, 'Oh Daddy, I was hungry for puha.' Then she began walking round and round the house, pressing her hands into her sides, pressing her hands. Later she went to bed and Dad delivered the girl.

My big sister Ngahuia brought the new little sister Maurea out into the kitchen where it was warm and began washing her. Then Mum called out to Dad that there was another baby and at first he thought it was all teka. He thought she was teasing because he had growled about her riding on the horse. But when he went to her he knew she wasn't playing after all and went to help, but the boy was stillborn. Mum was sad then because she had been riding on the horse so close to her time, but my father was good to her and said no, it was because the boy was too small. They took the tiny body up to where the old place had been, and buried it there with the other babies that had not lived.

Maurea was never very strong and on most nights we went to sleep listening to the harsh sound of her coughing. That was until she was about five years old. Then our parents took her to an old aunt of ours who knew about sicknesses, and the old aunt pushed her long forefinger down our sister's throat and hooked out lump after lump of hard knotted phlegm. Maurea was much better from then on, though still prone to chest complaints and has never been sturdy like the rest of us.

There were three different places where we went for kai moana. The first, about a mile round the beach, called Huapapa, was a place of small lagoons and rock pools. The rocks here were large and flat and extended well out into the sea. This was a good place for kina and paua and pupu. We would ride the horses out as far as we could and tether them to a rock. They would stand there in the sun and go to sleep.

To get kina, we would go out to where the small waves were breaking, in water about knee-deep. We'd peer into the water, turning the flat stones over, and it wouldn't take long to fill a sugar-bag with kina. The paua were there too, as well as in the rock pools further towards the shore. The younger children who were not old enough to stand in the deeper water, and not strong enough to turn the big rocks for paua and kina, would look about in the rock pools for pupu, each one of them hoping to find the biggest and the best.

The next place, Karekare, further round the beach, was also a good place for shellfish, but the reason we liked to go there was that there was a small lagoon with a narrow inlet, which was completely cut off from the sea at low tide. Often at low tide there were fish trapped there in the lagoon. And we children would all stand around the edge of the lagoon and throw rocks at the fish.

'Ana! Ana!' we'd yell. 'Patua! Patua!' hurling the stones into the water.

And usually there would be at least one fish floating belly up in the lagoon by the time we'd finished. Whoever jumped in first and grabbed it would keep it and take it home.

One day after a week of rain we arrived at Karekare to find the water in the lagoon brown and murky, and even before we got down from the horses we could see two dozen or more fins circling, breaking the surface of the water. We all got off the horses and ran out over the rocks calling, 'Mango, mango,' and scrambled everywhere looking for rocks and stones to throw. But my father came out and told us to put the rocks down. Then he walked out into the lagoon and began reaching into the water. Suddenly he threw his arms up, and there was a shower of water, and a shark came spinning through the air, 'Mango, mango,' way up over our heads with its white belly glistening and large drops of water raining all over us. 'Mango, mango,' we shouted. Then – smack! It landed threshing on the rocks behind us. So we hit it on the head with a stone to make sure of it, and turned to watch again. My father caught ten sharks this way, grabbing their tails and sending them arcing out over our heads to the rocks behind, with us all watching and shouting out 'Mango, mango,' yelling and jumping about on the rocks.

The other place, Waiariki, is very special to me. Special because it carries my name, which is a very old name and belonged to my grandfather and to others before him as well. It is a gentle quiet place where the lagoons are always clear and the brown rocks stand bright and sharp against the sky. This was a good place for crayfish and agar. Mum was the one who usually went diving for crayfish, ruku koura. She would walk out into the sea fully clothed and lean down into the water, reaching into the rock holes and under the shelves of rock for the koura. Sometimes she would completely submerge, and sometimes we would see just a little bit of face where her mouth was, sitting on top of the sea.

The rest of us would feel round in the lagoons for agar. Rimurimu we called it. For the coarse agar we would need to go out to where there was some turbulence in the water, to pluck the hard strands from the rocks. But the finest rimurimu was in the still parts of the lagoons and we would feel round for it with our feet and hands, and pick it and put it into our sugar-bags.

When our bags were full we would take the agar ashore and spread it on the sand to dry. Then we'd put it all into a big bale and tramp it down. We had a big frame of timber to hold the bale, and our own stencil to label it with. I don't know how much we were paid for a bale in those days. But I do remember once, after one of the cheques had arrived, my father went to town and came home in a taxi with a rocking horse and two guitars. He handed me one of the guitars and I tuned it up and strummed on it, and I remember thinking that it was the most beautiful sound I had ever heard.

And another time my father brought home a radio, and after that our neighbours and relations used to come every week to listen to *Gentleman Rider* or the *Hit Parade*. And when the boxing or wrestling was on, people would come from everywhere. We'd all squeeze into our kitchen and turn the radio up as loud as it would go. On the morning after the fight we boys would go down to the beach and find thick strands of bull kelp and make our own boxing belts and organise our own boxing or wrestling tournaments on the sand.

The horses were very useful to us then. They were of more use to us than a car or truck would have been. Besides using them for excursions round the beach, we used them for everyday work, and when the rains came and flooded the creek our horses were the only means we had of getting to town. All of our wood for the range was brought down from the hills by the horses too.

On the days when we were to go for firewood we boys would go up back before breakfast and bring the horses down, and after breakfast we'd prepare the horses for the day's work. Dad would sort out all the collars and chains, and we'd go out into the yard, put the collars on the horses, and hook the long coils of chain onto the hames. The we'd get together the axes and slashers and start out down and across the creek, and go up on to the scrub-covered hills about a mile from the house.

It was always the younger boys' job to trim the leaves and side branches from the felled manuka and stack the wood on to the track ready to be chained into loads for the horses to pull. One of the older boys who had been chopping would come down and wrap the short chains round the stacks, then hook the long chains from either side of the horses' collars on to each side of the load.

Once when I was about nine years old my father and mother were at the bottom of the hill stacking the wood into cords – we were selling wood then – for the trucks to come and take away to town. My older brothers were chopping and stacking at the top of the hill, and my sisters and I were taking the horses down with the loads. I was on my way up the hill on Blue Pony and my sister was at the top hitching a load to Punch, who was a good willing horse but very shy. Erana accidentally bumped the chain spreader against Punch's leg and away he went. I saw Punch coming, bolting towards me with the chains flying, but it was too late to do anything. Punch knocked Blue Pony down, and I went hurtling out over the bank like Dad's mango thrown out of the lagoon.

I landed in scrub and fern and wasn't hurt. Everyone came running to look at me, but I got up laughing, and I remember my father saying, 'E tama, that one flying!' Then he went off to rescue Punch, who was by then caught up in one of the fences by his chains.

On warm nights we used to like to go fishing for shark from the beach. Mangoingoi. We'd go down to the beach with our lines and bait and light a big fire there, and on some nights, especially when the sea was muddy after rain and we knew the sharks would be feeding close to the shore, there would be people spread out all along the beach, and four or five fires burning and cracking in the night.

We always used crayfish for bait, and because crayfish flesh is so soft we would bind it to our hooks with light flour-bag string. Then we would tie the ends of our lines to a log and prepare the remainder so that the full length of it would be used once it was thrown. We'd walk out into the sea then, twirling the end of the line with the hooks and horseshoe on it, faster and faster, then let it go. And the line would go zipping out over the sea, and sometimes by the fire's light we'd see the splash out offshore where the horseshoe sinker entered the water.

We waited after that, sitting up on the beach with our lines tied to our wrists. We'd talk, or sometimes sleep, and after a long while, usually an hour or more, someone's line would shoot away with shark.

'Mango, mango!'

'Aii he mango!'

And we would all tie our lines and go running to the water's edge, 'Mango, mango,' to watch the shark being pulled in with its tail flapping and water splashing everywhere.

Mum used to cut the shark into thick pieces and boil it, then skin it. Then she'd put it into a pan to cook with onions, and we'd eat till we were groaning. Sometimes we would hang strips of dark flesh on the line to dry, and when this had dried out we would put it in the embers of our outside fire to cook.

There was one teacher at school who used to get annoyed when we'd been eating dried shark at lunchtime. He'd march around the classroom flinging the windows open and saying, 'You kids have been eating shark again. You pong.' And we'd sniff around at each other, wondering what all the fuss was about.

Dad used to hang the shark liver on the line too, and let the oil drip into the stomach bag. Then he'd put the oil in a bottle and save it to treat the saddles and bridles with.

I went back to the old place last summer and took my wife and children with me for a holiday. I wanted them to know the quiet. I wanted them to enjoy the peace, and to do the things we used to do.

In most ways the holiday was all I hoped it would be. My parents still live there in much the same way as before, even though the house seems somewhat empty now with only the two of them and two grandsons living there. Most of the other families have moved away. The vegetable gardens are not as extensive now because there is not the need, but flowers and trees are as abundant as ever, and the summer house is still there with my father's ferns flourishing and the begonias blooming.

Electricity hasn't reached that far yet, so it is still necessary for the old people to bring the wood down from the hills, and I don't like to think of them doing this on their own with only two small boys to help.

My wife and children had a good holiday. We spent two days getting firewood so that there would be plenty there after we had gone. Punch, Blue Pony, Creamy and Crawford are all dead now, and the two horses that they use are getting old too. There are other younger horses on the hills, but with no one to break them in they are completely wild.

I took my family up on the hills and we sat looking out over the sea. I told them about the whale I had once seen out past the point, and about the American fleet, all lit, going silently by.

And one night I took them down to the beach fishing, Mangoingoi. We caught a little shark too, and Mum cooked it for us in the old way and my father hung strips of it to dry and caught the oil in the stomach bag for the bridles and saddles.

Another day we all went round the beach for kai moana and, although the tides were good and the weather perfect, we were the only ones there on the beach that day. We visited all the favourite places and took something from each. And when we came to Waiariki, which even now I think of as my own special place, I told my children its name, and that it was special to me because I had that name and so had others before me. And my little boy said to me, 'Dad, why can't we stay here forever?' because he has the name as well.

But when we arrived at the first place with our knives and bags and kits and dismounted from the horses, and looked out over the rocks of Huapapa, which is the best place for kai moana, I felt an excitement in me. I wanted to reap in abundance. I wanted to fill the kits full of good food from the sea. And then I wanted to tell my children to put their kits down on the sand and mimi on them so that we would find plenty of good kai moana to take home. I wanted to say this to them but I didn't. I didn't because I knew they would think it unclean to mimi on their kits, and I knew they would think it foolish to believe that by so doing, their kits would be more full of seafood than if they hadn't.

And when we left the rocks with our kits only half filled I felt deep regret in me. I don't mean that I thought it was because of my children not christening their kits as we stood on the beach that we were unable to fill our bags that day. There are several reasons, all of them scientific, why the shellfish beds are depleted. And for the few people living there now, there is still enough.

No. My regret came partly in the knowledge that we could not have the old days back again. We cannot have the simple things. I cannot have them for my children and we cannot have full kits any more. And there was regret in me too for the passing of the innocence, for that which made me unable me to say to my children, 'Put your kits on the sand, little ones. Mimi on your kits and then wash them in the sea. Then we will find plenty. There will be plenty of good kai moana in the sea and your kits will always be full.'

Breathing

Tina Shaw

When my aunt asked if I'd come to stay with her at the beach, it seemed like perfect timing. She had just moved in with myself and my mother into the little cottage on Great North Road. It was very noisy at night with the traffic streaming past, the buses and the souped-up cars, and my aunt said she couldn't think. Neither could I. I'd just moved back in with my mother after breaking up with Robert. The little cottage was really only good for one person.

My aunt, Bea, had recently burned her house down. It was an accident, she kept telling us. Her mobility scooter, which had been parked in the garage, had somehow ignited and set the place alight. Bea had walked away with nothing but the flannelette nightie she'd been wearing. It was lucky, said my mother drily, that she hadn't been wearing something more flammable.

Bea is older than my mother, and has always liked to think of herself as eccentric.

Her old buddy Max at the RSA had a house by the beach which he said Bea could live in while the insurance people looked at the claim. My aunt didn't drive (except for combustible mobility scooters), so she wanted me to come too. The house, we discovered, was at a remote beach on private property up north. Max had had it for years; it had been passed down through his family. He hardly ever used it, he said. She'd be doing him a favour.

The morning of our departure, my mother loaded up my car with all the things she thought Bea and I would need in what she imagined was a dilapidated shack on the edge of a marsh (my mother didn't have a high opinion of Bea's friends down at the RSA).

There was a box of canned goods; sheets and towels; suncream, mosquito repellent, cockroach powder. There were three second-hand, but perfectly good dresses my mother didn't want any more for Bea to wear. There was an old plastic kettle and a sharp knife. There was a jar of kitchen utensils.

The car rattled with all these things as I drove north on the motorway.

Bea's friend had drawn us a map with various directions in spidery writing: two hours past such-and-such town. Take eastern highway until you reach such-and-such turn-off. Drive until end of road, go through two gates. Take track on left. Three miles. Blue house.

I've left out the useful details, as I don't want anybody else finding this beach. It was a perfect, pristine beach, so unreal it seemed to have been magically created just for the two of us, for our mutual recuperation. It would have disappointed my mother to know there was no marsh, and apart from a nest of starlings under the eaves, the house was intact.

We climbed out of the car in a swirl of dust, and stood on the patch of buffalo grass, looking at the blue-glazed ocean and the smooth curve of pink sand.

'Well,' said Bea.

I didn't know what to say, either. 'We'd better unload the car.'

'All right, dear,' said Bea, digging around in her oversize handbag to find the key. 'I'll just have a little lie-down while you do that.'

Last week I turned 28. I've got long skinny legs, like a model, but too many freckles to be called photogenic. Also, my hair is ginger, which lots of people don't seem to like; it's not very fashionable at the moment to be ginger. It also doesn't help that I work at the museum, where everything is ordered, classified, and even the lighting is regulated. When I tell people at parties what I do their eyes glaze over. None of this, however, seemed to matter to Robert.

It all began because of the sleep apnoea.

My job at the museum was a public relations role. The job came with a uniform and a nifty hat. All I had to do was stroll around the museum, making myself available to lost or bewildered visitors. There were quite a few of them. Even with large arrows painted on the floor showing you where to go, the museum had many rooms and hallways and it was easy to get lost. You could end up in Chinese ceramics when you really wanted to find the interactive science display. It took me a week to find my way around.

I had a chair, as well, where I could sit and rest my feet. It was against the wall opposite the prehistoric skull case. It was quiet there, mainly because kids weren't interested in prehistoric skulls, and the lights were dim to create the right atmosphere. I'd sit in my chair and the next thing I'd know it was an hour later. This happened every afternoon. Then one day a young man holding a sketchbook was standing in front of me.

'You were asleep,' he said. 'Are you supposed to sleep on the job?'

I couldn't tell if he was being rude or funny. He had hair which fell over his forehead, and large lips. His skin looked very smooth, as if he used moisturiser.

'Can I help you with something, sir?' I asked, standing up and straightening my hat.

His name was Robert and even though he was 31, he was still at varsity, studying anthropology. He followed me around for the rest of the afternoon, as I helpfully pointed various lost people in the right direction. His thesis project concerned a gentle, tree-dwelling people from the Solomon Islands. They had had quite pale skin and worshipped the trees as well as living in them.

'What happened to them?' I asked.

'Oh, they got slaughtered by a sea-faring tribe who cut down all their trees to build ground dwellings.'

He said it in such a matter-of-fact way that I felt dizzy for a moment, and leaned against the glass case that displayed Maori greenstone. He took my elbow, as if I might faint. We were close together in the dim museum light, his eyes the same deep jade as the pieces on display, when the closing bell went. We both looked up, startled.

'Would you like to go for a drink?' he asked.

'All right,' I said.

Later, when we were saying goodnight, he said I ought to see a doctor.

Our days at the beach settled into a rhythm. Bea had set up two chairs out the front of the house, and every evening around five we would sit in these chairs and sip the heady vodka concoctions which Bea mixed in her cocktail shaker. They tasted like fruit drinks, but that was entirely deceptive. The chillybin, where Bea kept the vodka and various other bottles, sat between the chairs. I didn't like to enquire too much into the contents of the bottles. If I didn't know what I was drinking, then I could keep pretending they were fruit drinks.

We watched the sea lapping at the pearly sand. Once, a dolphin leapt out of the water. It happened so quickly I thought I'd imagined it. Bea was smiling in that dazed, beatific way she gets after several of her cocktails. I don't know if she even saw it.

Eventually, I'd stagger into the house and fetch crackers and cheese. It was all we could manage for supper. The real cooking I did during the day when it wasn't so easy to drop things or burn myself.

'It's a funny old life,' said Bea. Her hands were folded on her lap; she was wearing one of the dresses my mother had discarded. It was pastel blue, with straps and a handkerchief hemline. Her bare legs were crossed, and all the veins and creases were visible.

'Yes?' I said.

The sea was pouting tonight, like a sulky teenager. Perhaps it was going to rain soon. An odd calm had fallen over the waves, and the surface of the water looked oily.

'There's you,' said Bea, 'up and leaving your young man ...'

'I don't want to talk about Robert,' I said quickly.

But she carried on as if I hadn't spoken. 'And there's your mother ...' She started humming then; perhaps she'd drift off to sleep soon and I wouldn't have to hear any more of her misguided attempts at family analysis. 'There's me too, of course, must include myself.' I wondered if there would be a point coming soon. She gave me a knowledgable glance. 'It's a line, don't you see? Like an inheritance. Like heart disease.'

She sighed then, looking out to sea. I, too, studied the sea, looking for clues.

'You don't have to accept your inheritance,' she murmured softly.

I moved in with Robert on the day Edmund Hillary died. It was a Friday.

There was a sudden hailstorm as we were carrying my things, my boxes and suitcases inside. I stood on the veranda, arms folded across my ribs, thinking about omens, while the hail whitened the lawn. Robert was grinning, pleased with the hail. He put his arm around my waist and said, 'How about that!' I tried to compose my face: I couldn't tell him about the deep foreboding which had arrived with the hail. Although, in hindsight, perhaps it was really the news about Hillary that had done it.

We went inside, and had cups of tea at the small table in the kitchen and ate slices of toast with Marmite on top. I had never lived with a man before. There had been guys, sure, and one or two of them had wanted to live with me, but somehow I'd always put them off. Eventually something would happen and these guys would drop off, as if silently slipping over the edge of a cliff. I wouldn't ever see them again; not even waiting for a bus, or waiting in line at the supermarket.

But Robert was different. He wouldn't take no for an answer. He'd put his arm around my waist and ask me what I liked to eat for breakfast, and did I prefer to wash my whites separately from my colours, and would I like to grow some vegetables? Often, we'd lie on his bed in the dark (this was before I moved in), the room lit by the orange streetlight outside, and he would tell me anthropology stories. How the Hmong hill tribe used to support themselves by growing opium poppies, but now they sold needlework; and how the Karen people of Burma lived in bamboo houses raised up on stilts with the pigs and cows living underneath.

The stories soothed me somehow. I liked to think of all those peoples out there in the world, getting on with their lives. And I thought if I lived with Robert, it would be like that all the time: stories lulling me to sleep, like being rocked in a dinghy on a gentle sea and his murmuring voice the last thing I heard each night.

But Robert had his thesis to write, and liked to work on it late into the night. And then, I was so tired from walking around the museum all day, that I'd be asleep by nine, without even trying. The doctor had given me sleeping tablets; Robert thought it was sleep apnoea.

'There are times in the night,' he told me, 'when you stop breathing. Then you sort of gasp, and start breathing again.'

That frightened me so badly I wanted to stay awake – I didn't want to succumb to sleep. But it always got me in the end, like a drug I didn't know I'd taken. 'You must shake me,' I told Robert, 'if it happens again.'

'Okay,' he said in his usual cheerful way.

The next night I was dreaming of being trapped underground, like those miners in Australia, and then Robert was shaking me. '*What?*' I cried. '*What is it?*'

'You did it again,' he said, rolling back over to sleep. 'You asked me to shake you,' he muttered.

I lay awake, staring at the orangey tongue-and-groove ceiling, remembering the hail. I just couldn't carry on like this. I didn't like being shaken awake, after all, and I missed the Robert I'd known when we were simply going out together.

That weekend I moved back out. Robert stood on the veranda, arms by his sides, looking hurt. I'll call, I said through the open car window. But mentally I was seeing Robert sliding off the edge of an abyss.

Lying face down on the beach, I could see that the sand was comprised of tiny pink shells. Minute, miniscule, pearly-pink. So that's why it was the colour it was, this sand. I sat up and crossed my legs, pleased I'd resolved that one. Waves chugged relentlessly in and out. The sun moved behind a cloud and shadows raced across the surface of the sea.

Bea was up to her knees in the water, her skirt bobbing in the swell, working her toes into the sand. She held a plastic bucket in her hand, but it looked like she was doing the twist. Every now and then she'd turn round and cry out, 'Found another one!' Then she'd stick her arm into the water, up to the shoulder, and pull out a tuatua, holding it aloft for me to see. We were going to make fritters before we started drinking.

My sleeping was much improved since coming to this beach. The drinking seemed to help. I had had a polysomnogram and the doctor had booked me in for an operation, so that I wouldn't keep dying and reviving during the night. Really, things were looking okay.

Except there was a little Robert-shaped stone inside me. Sometimes I'd take out my cellphone and look at it, just like I could take out the Robert-shaped stone and look at that. But no matter how much I turned the stone, or the phone, the answer was always the same.

'Found another one!' Bea cried triumphantly.

I wiped the tears off my face, gave a brave smile, and waved.

'What I *meant* to say,' Bea said into the mutual silence, as if continuing a conversation we'd been having all along, 'is that your mother got hurt, so she hid herself away. Completely natural response, of course. Your father, bless him, gambled all his money on the pokies. Sent them both broke.' Bea took a meditative sip of her cocktail. It was an orange concoction this evening, to match the sunset. 'But it doesn't mean that *you* have to follow suit, too.'

A pressing feeling came into my chest, like somebody holding the palm of their hand against my breastbone. 'It's got nothing to do with my mum, or dad,' I said.

'No no, I'm sure it hasn't,' said Bea. 'Nonetheless. There is such a thing as breaking free.'

The orangeade sea was jaunty tonight; the sun had gone down behind the sheep hills which stood beyond the house. The sky went on into hazy infinity. It ought to have been a beautiful sight, but I wasn't in the mood. I left my glass on the ground, and went inside the house. Lying on the lumpy old mattress, I listened to the sussuration of the sea. The house was growing dark, and my breathing filled my head. Eventually, I heard Bea's apologetic footsteps coming across the kitchen floor and pausing in my doorway. I hadn't actually shut the door, so maybe I wanted her comfort after all.

'Never mind me, love,' she muttered, 'I'm just an old woman.'

I squeezed shut my eyes, then wanted to protest, *No you're not!* But the doorway was empty.

My dad wasn't that bad, really. He just loved the thrill of winning. But you had to keep playing, and playing, and playing, to keep getting that thrill. And when it got hold of him, he became another person; he became a person who couldn't walk away, even when he was losing money and the winning had become a myth that happened to somebody else. He became overwhelmed by a force much bigger than himself.

This was how Mum tried to explain it to me as we walked through Eden Gardens to plant the hebe and the brass plaque she'd had made for him. She stumbled once, over a tree root, like an old person, and I had to grab her elbow so she wouldn't fall. Her eyes, turning to me, were grateful, though I don't think she'd even noticed the stumble.

'I met him at a party, you know,' she was saying, as I held her elbow and we carried on along the path beneath dusty rhododendrons, 'and as soon as I met him, I knew, this was the one for me.' A little, indulgent laugh. 'Isn't that silly?' I steered her clear of another tree root. 'I mean, how silly is that ...' Tears were leaking now, down her cheeks, but I don't think she noticed.

We planted the hebe in the spot they'd shown us; in front of a bench, in a bed which overlooked another, lower part of the garden. Groundcover plants grew in that lower garden, and a lovely scent, like incense, rose up from them. Then I stuck the plaque in the ground next to the hebe, and we stood there for a long time just looking at it.

Finally, my mother shook her head, as if dismissing all that as a bad lot – my dad, her marriage, all the lost money – and we went off to the garden café and had a cup of tea.

I walked along the lacy edge of the waves, my bare feet crushing tiny pink shells underfoot, and switched on my cellphone. The sound of the waves was loud in my ears; or it could have been the sound of my heart. I'd have the operation. I'd talk to Robert. Perhaps I'd get a new job, a job where I didn't get lost among antiquities, where I didn't have to dig myself out. I would've told all of these things to Robert right then, except there was no reception for my phone.

The sea tipped a wave across my feet. I looked up to see a dolphin break the smooth surface of the water, then it splashed back down again as if nothing at all had happened.

Piha Dunny Do

Fay Weldon

Piha Beach is the pride of the Waitakere Ranges, on the west coast of Auckland; the ranges are the pride of wilderness lovers everywhere. Tasman breakers crash against a wild shore, native New Zealand bush –grave, deep green and silent – is re-born on windswept hills, pohutukawa trees line the shore, red blooms against black spume-flayed rock, and the local council imposes strict rules on anyone trying to buy and live here. Buy ten acres, and be allowed to build on only 800 square feet of it. You won't get to see your neighbors easily, though they're friendly enough if you can find them. The blokes are brain surgeon types, or airline pilots or potters, the gals likewise. All genders do yoga, flirt with the arts. Marin County in California, in style and sophistication, is the nearest comparison I can think of to the Waitakeres. Don't drive on the beaches, please: don't break the spell. Human footprints only. Lucky are they that live here, in this area west of Auckland, New Zealand, the World, the Solar System, the Universe. Theirs is the kingdom of nature, and the best that civilization can provide as well, all within commuting distance of Auckland's restaurants, theatres, and major hairdressers.

Aficionados rate Piha highly; a surfers' beach; fine black sand in a perfect curve contains a hammering, moody sea, the curve melting to soft green sward. There's a craggy island just off shore, and great waves on a good day. When I was here for the 'Dunny Do' there was an exemplary sunset, together with a rising harvest moon, the last remaining surfers, young males with bronzed and gleaming muscles, were walking out of the sea like Gods.

The Dunny Do was a fund-raising event. A dunny, in the Antipodes, is what further north is euphemistically called a toilet, a loo, a lavatory, a WC, a john, a powder room, a comfort station, or more graphically a shit house. Dunny's a good word for it, both basic and polite, with a healthy outdoor flavour: it feels safe – here in New Zealand, at any rate, if not in Australia. In the Land of Oz, the dunny is traditionally home to the dreaded redback spider which leaps out of its depths to bite you on your private parts and kill you most painfully. But this is Kiwiland, and there is nothing here to kill or corrupt, not as much as a poisonous snake. The bush and beaches of New Zealand are benign. Mind you, the ground beneath your feet seems more firmly fixed to the core of the earth in Australia than it does in New Zealand, where it tends to shake and tremble rather with volcano and earthquake.

A 'do', in the Antipodes, is any formal occasion you dress up for, exchanging trainers for heels and track suits for fitted garments, where nibbles and drinks are served. On this occasion, the Piha Library Dunny Do, I was the entertainment on offer, a writer on tour, with a new book to read from, friends in the area and a New Zealand childhood to talk about.

Piha library is a small elegant building set four-square in the middle of the beach where sward meets sand, and if you can find me a library equal to it in views anywhere in the world, tell me. Its only failing was that it did not at the time have a dunny, let alone a septic tank. The Dunny Do was to remedy this.

This spring, coincidentally, I was back in Piha, fresh off the flight from London, to cut the ribbon for the completed toilet block, required to be the first to give the bowl a celebratory flush. This was not the first toilet block I have opened. (Others get to launch ships and open museums, I seem to get the more basic civic duties. Last time had been in Colet Park in Shepton Mallet, Somerset. As ever, a most badly needed civic amenity. Just how bad I could tell because of the little girl who jumped up and down beside me even as I snipped, tugging at my sleeve. 'Can I go please, Miss, now, Miss. Oh please hurry Miss!' I did what I could to hurry but the scissors provided for cutting ribbons are often blunt, rootled as they are from a back drawer in some council office at the last moment, and these were no exception. I struggled with the fraying silk but finally just lifted the ribbon and let her in under it. The ceremony's the thing).

Next it was to be the dunny at Piha Beach, and next year I am to cut the ribbon for the new powder rooms at Bromley House Subscription Library in Nottingham, of which I am President. *Noblesse oblige*. We've all got to go.

Kenneth's Friend

Owen Marshall

At the north side, towards the point, the shore was rocky. When the tide was going out I liked to search the pools for butterfish and flat crabs like cardboard cut-outs, sea snails with plates instead of heads, and flowing anemone in pink and mauve. Once Kenneth let a rock fall on my hand there on purpose, after I told him I didn't want to spend the morning making papier-mache figures. He said it was an accident of course, but I knew he meant it. The rock had a hundred edges of old accretions, and cut like glass. I sat and waited for the sun to stop the cuts bleeding. I thought about Kenneth and me, and how I came to be there at all.

I had good friends when I lived in Palmerston North, friends that experience had shown the value of, but when we shifted to Blenheim I didn't have time to make friends before the holidays. I liked Robbie Macdonald best. He and I became closer later, but Kenneth seemed to attach himself to me in those first weeks. Perhaps he felt it gave him at least a temporary distinction to be seen with the new boy. He came home with me often after school, and lent me *Crimson Comet* magazines.

At Christmas time he invited me to go with his family to their holiday home in Queen Charlotte Sound. His father was a lawyer and mayor of the town. My mother was pleased I'd been invited, and for sixteen days too. She gave me a crash course on table manners and guest etiquette. I had a ten shilling note in an envelope so that I could buy something for Kenneth's parents before I left.

The house had a full veranda along the front, facing out towards the bay. We used to have meals there, and standing out like violin music from amongst the talk of the Kinlethlys and their guests, I could hear the native birds in the bush, and the waves on the beach. It was a millionaire's setting in any country but ours, though Mr Kinlethly was a lawyer and mayor of the town admittedly. Glow-worms too; there were glow-worms under the cool bank of the stream. At night I crept out to see them, hanging my head over the bank, and with my arms in the creek to hold me up. The earth in the bush was soft and fibrous. I could plunge my hands into it without stubbing the fingers. The sand of the small bay was cream where it was dry, and yellow closer to the water. There was no driftwood, but sometimes after rough weather there would be corpses of bull kelp covered with flies, and filigree patterns of more fragile seaweed pressed in the sand.

What Kenneth wanted, I found out, wasn't a friend, but someone to boss about. A sort of young brother, without the inconvenience of his sharing any parental affection. With no natural authority at school, Kenneth made the most of his position at the bay. Each night before we went to bed, Kenneth enjoyed the privilege of choosing his bunk and so underlined his superiority. He might bounce on the top bunk for a while, then say that he'd chosen the bottom one; he might wait until I'd put my pyjamas on one of them, then he'd toss my pyjamas off and say he'd decided to sleep there himself. He liked to play cards and Monopoly for hours on end, or work on his shell collection. Whenever we had a disagreement as to what we should do, Kenneth would say that I could go home if I didn't like it. I think in a way that's what Kenneth wanted – for me to say that I wanted to go home, that I couldn't stick it out. He didn't understand how much the bay offered me, despite its ownership. Kenneth's parents didn't know we disliked each other. We carried on our unequal struggle within the framework of their expectations. We slept together, and set off in the mornings to play together, we didn't kick each other at the table, or sulk to disclose our feud. His parents were always there however, as a final recourse: the reason I had to come to heel and follow him back to the house when he saw fit, or help him catalogue his shells in the evening instead of watching the glow-worms.

The Kinlethlys seemed to take their bay for granted, corrupted by the ease and completeness of their ownership. Mr Kinlethly was away more days than he was there, and at night he shared the family enthusiasm for cards. I never saw him walk into the bush, and he went fishing only once or twice, a sort of tokenism. There was no doubt he was pleased with the place though. He liked visitors so that they could praise it, and I heard him telling Mrs Kinlethly that the property had appreciated seven hundred percent since he purchased it. Mrs Kinlethly had some reservations I think. She wouldn't allow any uncleaned fish near the house. She said the smell lingered. We would gut them at the shore, washing the soft flaps of their bellies in the salt water, and tossing their entrails to the gulls. Mrs Kinlethly gave us what she called the filleting board, and we would scale and dismember the blue cod and terakihi in the ocean they came from, the filleting board between Kenneth and me, our feet stretching into the ripples. Mrs Kinlethly seemed sensitive to the smell of fish. When the wind was strong from the sea, blowing directly up to the house, she said it smelled of fish. It didn't really. It carried the smell of kelp, sand-hoppers, mussels, jetty timber, island farms, distant horizons – and fish.

One wall of Kenneth's room was covered with the display case for his shells, and our bunks were on the opposite side. I thought the collection interesting at first, the variety of colours and shapes, the neatly typed documentation. Each entry seemed to have one sentence beginning 'This specimen ...' Mr Kinlethly wrote them out, and Kenneth proudly typed them on the special stickers, which I got to lick. 'This specimen a gift from Colonel L.S.Gilchrist following a visit to our bay,' or, 'This specimen one of the few examples with mantle intact'. The collection seemed to admirably satisfy the two Kinlethly requirements concerning possessions – display and investment.

My dislike of the shells began when I had sunstroke. Kenneth and I had been collecting limpets on the rocks, and I forgot to wear a hat. The sun on the back of my neck all morning was too much for me. I lay on the bottom bunk, and tried not to think of the bowl Mrs Kinlethly had placed on a towel by the bed. The family considered it rather inconsiderate of me to get sick. After all I was there to keep Kenneth amused, not to add to Mrs Kinlethly's workload. I lay there trying not to be a bother, and hearing Kenneth's laugh from the veranda. In the late afternoon Mr Kinlethly brought a guest back from Picton, and they came in to see the shells. 'A friend of Kenneth's,' said Mr Kinlethly as my introduction. I was bereft of any more original name at the bay. It was always 'Kenneth's friend'. 'I think he's been off-colour today,' said Mr Kinlethly. 'Now here's one in particular; the Cypraea argus.'

'Oh yes.'

'And Olivia cryptospira.'

'Strikingly formed, isn't it?'

'Cassis cornuta.'

I wanted to be sick. The nerves in my stomach trampolined, and saliva flooded my mouth. The mixing bowl on the towel seemed to blossom before me. Mr Kinlethly was in no hurry. 'Most in this other section were collected locally,' he said. 'Kenneth is a very assiduous collector, and also people around the Sounds have become aware of our interest. A surprising number of shells come as gifts.' Despite myself I looked over at the shells. Many of them seemed to have the sheen of new bone; like that revealed when you turn the flesh away from the shoulder, or knuckle of a newly killed sheep. I had to discipline myself, so that I wasn't sick until Mr Kinlethly and his visitor had left the room. The shells were always different to me after that.

The Kinlethlys had a clinker-built dinghy. It always had a little bilge water in it that smelled of scales and bait. They had their own boatshed for it even, just like a garage, with folding doors so that the dinghy could be pulled in, and a hand-winch at the back of the shed to do it with. The dinghy was never put in the shed while I was there. Kenneth said they left it out all summer. We used it to pull it up the sand a way, and then take out the anchor and push one of the flukes in the ground in case of a storm, or freak tide. Using the dinghy was probably the best thing of all. When we went fishing I could forget the boring times, like playing Monopoly, and helping Kenneth with his shells. I could look down the woven cord of the hand line, seeing how the refraction made it veer off into the green depths, and I could listen to the water slapping against the sides of the dinghy. Closer to the shore the sea was so clear that I could see orange starfish on the bottom, and the sculptured sand-dunes there, the sweeping outlines formed by the currents and not the wind. Flounders hid there, so successfully that they didn't exist until they moved, and vanished again when they stopped as if by some magician's trick.

Wonderful things happened at the bay, even though I was only Kenneth's friend. Like the time we were out in the dinghy and it began to rain. The water was calm, but the cloud pressed lower and lower, squeezing out what air remained between it and the sea, and then the rain began. I'd never been at sea in rain before. The cloud dipped down into the sea, and the water lay smooth and malleable beneath the impact of the drops.

The surface dimpled in the rain, and the darkest and closest of the clouds towed shadows which undulated like stingrays across the swell. 'I never think of it raining on the sea,' I said to Kenneth, 'Imagine it raining on whole oceans, and there's no one there.'

'Bound to happen,' said Kenneth. He couldn't see why I was in no hurry to get back.

'I always think of it raining on trees, animals, the roofs of cars,' I said weakly. I couldn't share with Kenneth the wonder that I felt.

Kenneth had no respect for confidences. That evening at tea, when Mrs Kinlethly told the others how wet he and I had got in the dinghy, Kenneth said that I'd wanted to stay out and see the rain. 'He didn't know that rain fell on the sea as well as on the land,' said Kenneth. That wasn't the whole truth of it, but it was no use saying anything. I just blushed, and Mrs Kinlethly laughed. Kenneth's father said, 'Sounds as if we have a real landlubber in our midst,' in a tone that implied he wasn't a landlubber. I learnt not to talk to Kenneth about anything that mattered.

On the Thursday of the second week there were dolphins again at the entrance to the bay. I admired dolphins more than anything else. They seemed set on a wheel, the highest point of which just let them break the surface before curving down into the depths. I imagined they did a complete cart-wheel down there in the green water, then came sliding up again, like a side-show. 'There's dolphins out at the point,' said Mr Kinlethly. Mr and Mrs Thomson and their two unmarried daughters were with us on Thursday.

'I've never seen dolphins,' said Mrs Thomson.

'Quite a school of them,' said Mr Kinlethly. He decided that his guests must make an expedition in the dinghy to see the dolphins. Mrs Kinlethly wouldn't go, but the Thomsons settled the dinghy well down in the water and there wasn't room for both Kenneth and me.

'There's not room for both the boys,' said Mrs Kinlethly. Kenneth didn't care about the dolphins, but he wasn't going to let me go. He called out that he wanted to go, and his father hauled him aboard.

'Kenneth's friend can come another time,' said Mrs Thomson vacuously, and the dinghy pulled away clumsily. I waded out a bit, and kicked around in the water to show I didn't care, but I could see Kenneth with his head partly down watching me, waiting to catch my eye, and with the knowing little grin he had when he knew I was hurt. The dinghy angled away towards even deeper water, the bow sweeping this way then that, with the uneven rowing of Mr Kinlethly and Mr Thomson.

'Dolphins here we come,' I heard Kenneth shouting in his high voice.

That finished it for me, not missing out on the dolphins, but Kenneth going merely because he knew I wanted to. I'd taken a good deal, because after all I was just a friend of Kenneth's invited for part of the holidays, but I was beginning to think myself pretty spineless. I thought of my Palmerston friends, and the short work they'd have made of Kenneth. I left Mrs Kinlethly watching the dinghy leave the shelter of the bay to reach the dolphins at the point. I went up to the house, across the wide, wooden veranda and into Kenneth's room. From the bottom bunk I took a pillow case, and began to fill it with shells from Kenneth's collection. I tried to remember the ones he and his father liked best, the ones most often shown to visitors. Pectern maximus, Bursa bubo, and Cassis cornuta, the yellow helmet. The heavy specimens I threw into the bag, and heard them crunch into the shells already there. Once committed to it, the enormity of the crime gave it greater significance and release. Whatever outrage the Kinlethlys might feel, whatever recompense they might insist on, Kenneth would understand: he'd know why it was done, and what it represented in terms of him and me.

I took the shells up the track into the bush, and I sat above the glow-worm creek and threw the shells into the creek bed, and into the bush around it. Most disappeared without sound, swallowed up in the leaves and tobacco soil. The yellow helmet stuck in the cleft of a tree, and as I sat guiltily in the coolness, and heard the ocean in the bay, it didn't seem incongruous to me, that Cassis cornuta set like a jewel in the branches. The bush was a good imitation of an ocean floor, or so I could imagine it anyway.

A sense of drabness followed the excitement of rebellion. I came down to the house, and replaced the pillow case. Without a plan I began to return to the beach, scuffling in the stones and listening to the sound of the sea. Mrs Kinlethly came up the path towards me. I thought she must have found out about the shells already, and her response was more than anything I'd expected. She walked with her hands crossed on her chest, as if keeping something there from escaping, and her tongue hung half out of her mouth. It was an obscenity, worse than if she'd opened her dress as she came. I tried not to look at her face, and I felt the muscles of my arms and shoulders tighten, like at school just before I was strapped. Mrs Kinlethly passed so close to me that I heard the leather of her sandals squeaking, but she didn't stop, or say anything. She went up the steps, and the house swallowed her up in complete silence. I couldn't work out what was happening. I sat down there by the path and waited. I looked out towards the bay and the drifting gulls, letting the wind bring the association of the sea to me.

Mr Kinlethly came up next, without his trousers and with everything else wet. Instead of his hair being combed across his head as usual, it hung down one side like an ice-plant, and the true extent of his baldness was revealed. 'The dinghy went over. Kenneth's gone,' he shouted at me forcefully, and looked about for others to tell. He seemed amazed that there was just me by the path in the sun, and the birds calling in the bush behind the house. His eyes searched for the crowds that should have been there to receive such news. When I made no reply, he turned away despairingly. 'Kenneth's gone. I must get to the phone,' he shouted at the monkey-puzzle tree by the veranda, and he strode into the house. His coloured shirt stuck to his back, and on the ankle of one white leg were parallel cuts from the rocks.

The house filled rapidly after Mr Kinlethly made his phone calls, until there were enough people even for him: relatives from both sides of the family, friends, and folk from the next bay. Two policemen from Picton came, quiet men who kept out of the house, and began the search for Kenneth. I rang my father when I could, and asked him to pick me up at the turn-off by four o'clock. My mother had made it very clear to me about thanking the Kinlethlys before I left, but the way it was I couldn't bring myself to say anything. I just packed my things, and walked up the road to wait for my father. I was up there by mid-afternoon, and I climbed up the bank above the road and sat there waiting. I hadn't had anything to eat since breakfast. I could see right over the bay, and although the house was hidden by the foreshortened slope and the bush, I could see the boatshed like a garage at the edge of the sand. Where the dinghy had capsized at the point, the chop was visible, occasional small white crests in the wind.

Why I Never Learned to Swim

David Lyndon Brown

The sea was a distant roar, simmering far away on the horizon, and the air boiled white above the hot black sand. I was building a battlement around the blanket where my mother lay, but the sand was dry and the turrets kept collapsing, invading the blanket, infiltrating the paper bag full of warm tomato sandwiches and the plastic tumblers sticky with raspberry cordial. It was impossible to restrict the sand to the beach. I lay down on my back staring straight at the sun until it turned black and then I got up and staggered around with my arms outstretched, like a blind boy. Then I looked at my mother for a while, waiting for her to come back into focus.

'I'm going for a walk,' I announced. 'I'm going exploring.'

'Well, don't go too far, and don't go in,' my mother said, turning over, slick with a home-made marinade of oil and vinegar.

The heat from the sand entered the soles of my roman sandals and rose up my legs as I headed towards the ocean. I walked with crossed legs, then hopped a bit, then galloped on one hand and one foot. Everyone would be astonished by these weird tracks and wonder what strange creature was at large on the beach.

Suddenly the sand dipped and the waves came thrashing in. They were tall and loud and kept hurling themselves down and then rushing out again. I dipped the toe of my sandal into the foam that had been spat up along the tide-line. It looked like the stuff that emptied out of my mother's washing machine, or what you sick up after too much lemonade. Further up the beach, I could see some children dashing in and out of the surf, and I walked slowly toward them, popping the beads of a seaweed necklace the sea had chucked out. The boys were brown and glossy in their little togs and sparks shot off them as they raced from the water. There was a man with them. A giant of a man. He grabbed the boys, swung them high into the air and launched them into the waves. Then he sat them astride his massive shoulders and cantered along the beach like a centaur. I stopped to watch. I was bewitched by that colossus and my eyes ranged over his body, his glistening limbs, coming to rest on the blue satin bulge between those mighty thighs. I sat down to unbuckle my sandals. Part of me wanted the man to rush over and sweep *me* off my feet, but I felt dry and opaque next to those luminous kids, and self-conscious in the matching shirt and shorts my mother had made out of a stupid old curtain. I took off the shirt and stuck it under my sandals. My skin was as pale as milk.

I was shuffling, up to my ankles in the water, sifting the sand through my toes, when the ball the boys were playing with plopped into the water in front of me.

'Get it,' they shouted. 'Get it before it goes out.' The red ball was bobbing in the trough between the towering waves. I waded towards it. Up to my knees. Up to my waist. And then suddenly the sand dropped away beneath me and I was under the water. I could see the red ball above me and, beyond it, the yellow ball of the sun. It was so quiet down there. I felt as though I was breathing underwater like a fish. I can swim, I thought, as the ocean sucked and dragged me. I'm swimming. I found my feet and staggered up into the air, but a wave bashed me and another tumbled me, rolling me along the bottom.

The hot sand burned my back. I was lying in a circle of upside-down boys. The big brown man was kissing me on the lips. I was pinned down by the pressure of his enormous hands on my chest. There was a halo of light around his head. I gazed up at him through my eyelashes and then turned and deposited a little pile of pink vomit onto the sand: tomato sandwiches, raspberry cordial.

'Let's go and find your Mummy,' the man said gently. I sat up, to disguise what was happening in my shorts.

'You'll have to carry me,' I whispered.

Syrup

Linda Niccol

The cover of the book, which featured a dramatic black-and-white photograph of an overturned jam jar, a teaspoon and a bumblebee, was impossible to ignore. I picked it up. *Syrup* was the title. The author, Norris Fairchild. Heart thudding, I turned to the first story and began to read.

Syrup described our first kiss, charmingly narrated by the bumblebee that brought us together. How clever, I thought, remembering Norris's gift for seeing the extraordinary in the ordinary.

It was the summer that the sand, not content with its huge expanse of beach and ocean floor, drifted into everything.

Nights were spent tossing and turning like the fairy-tale princess, as each grain seemed to grow to the size of a pea. During the days, mouthfuls of limp, overdressed salad were punctuated with an unpleasant crunchiness.

It wasn't long before the sand found its way inside me. Grit ran in my veins. Nothing felt right any more.

My parents, my mother in particular, had begun to embarrass me.

Wearing clothes that were far too young for her – tight cropped pants in bright 'fashion' colours that clung in all the wrong places. Her toenails gleamed like sticky lollies in her strappy, toe-strangling sandals. She dyed her hair an unnatural auburn. At the endless round of neighbourhood get-togethers, when people asked, as if I wasn't there, 'And how old is Ally now?' someone would smirk coyly at me and add, 'Sweet seventeen and never been kissed.'

As if to avoid these issues, my father would take refuge behind the barbecue, the cartoon breasts on his apron lending him the look of an unfortunate transvestite. Oblivious, he would wave his long fork over the slabs of steak and cheerfully stab sausages until they burst from their skins, misshapen and burnt. He'd pour me shandies which were mostly lemonade, and say brightly, 'Don't get tiddly now young lady.' Blissfully unaware that the gin in his cabinet was now mainly water.

My younger brother would point out what he considered were my physical defects to anyone who would listen.

'Look at her legs, aren't they fat,' Tom would shriek, his sun-bleached head bobbing as her jumped up and down gleefully. I would tense my thighs in the short summer dress my mother insisted I wear, and blush furiously.

Later, when there was no one around, I would creep up behind Tom and push him to the ground, pinning him down, my knees jammed into his arm muscles. His head would thrash frantically from side to side, lips tightly pursed, as I worked my mouth and let a long trail of saliva dribble down towards his desperate, screwed-up face. I would suck the saliva back into my mouth and then let another trail descend, the citrus scent of the grapefruit trees above us and the crushed grass below, pungent in my nostrils.

Most evenings I sat cocooned in the tall flax bushes anchoring the grass verge that rose above the beach, as far away from everyone as possible.

Hugging my secret close. The smoke from the dying barbecue fire drifted across the lawn. The sun sank slowly into the sea, pulling the pink blanket of the sky down over it. The voices of my family rose and fell with the clatter of cutlery, a reminder that I could never truly escape them. Yet.

'Seen anyone you like more than yourself lately?' asked my grandfather, coming up behind me as the light faded. It was the question he often asked, and as usual we both laughed when I protested.

'Only you, Grandad.'

He patted my shoulder and we watched the sea shift from aqua to dimpled grey. It was the first time I'd ever lied to him.

Until that summer Norris Fairchild and I had lived in parallel universes. Our families knew each other by sight. We lived in close-by suburbs; we spent our holidays at the beach within two streets of each other. We went to the same schools. For a while we even attended the same non-charismatic Baptist church, until the more conservative Fairchilds must have decided the new woman minister wasn't for them and switched to high Anglican. Mrs Fairchild would smile and nod at my mother in the supermarket, rather like a queen acknowledging one of her subjects. My father was a car salesman and Norris's a merchant banker; the line of wealth was one our parents did not cross.

One sultry afternoon I dawdled down the seaside street where Norris and his family spent the holidays. Sprinklers whirred on front lawns, small rainbows shone in their rain. The heat rose off the tar in waves. Norris appeared in the distance like a mirage, holding something that flashed in the sunlight. As I got closer I saw he was holding a jar full of watery liquid and a teaspoon. He knelt down on the pavement in front of a bedraggled, flightless bumblebee, and spooned some of the liquid onto the pavement.

'Drink up,' he said, waving the silver spoon like a wand. 'You'll feel much better.'

My shadow fell over him. He looked up, shielding his eyes with his bony-wristed hands, nail-bitten fingers blunt-tipped.

'Hi, Ally. I'm just trying to get him in the air again. Sometimes bees lose energy. Four million wing flaps and it's all over. Sugar and watery syrup helps.'

Surprised and elated that Norris remembered my name, I squatted and looked at the bee, its mandibles and front legs moving feebly at the edge of the puddle of sticky syrup.

'How long does it take to work?' I asked, leaning closer, breathing in the body-warmed scent of laundry detergent in his freshly-washed T-shirt.

'Depends. Sometimes it doesn't. Worth a try, though.' His large, pale-lashed grey eyes narrowed to slits. His mouth twitched and curved into an uncertain smile. An invisible hand reached into my chest and turned a handle. I smiled back and stood up quickly, the blood rushing in my ears. Dizzy, I sat on the bottom step of the short flight that led to his parents' beach house. The texture of the sun-warmed step, bowed with years of footsteps, was pleasant beneath my bare thighs.

Norris sat beside me. Together we watched the bee's progress.

'What are you doing next year?' he asked.

'Journalism probably. If I get in.' I picked at a clump of scraggly mauve and white flowers clinging to a crack in the concrete. Noticing the hairs I'd missed this morning with my father's razor, I crossed my legs.

'Here? In Wellington, I mean?' he asked, swirling the syrup around in the jar, the spoon clanking against the sides.

'I'm not sure yet. Auckland, or maybe Christchurch. I've applied for all the courses. What about you?'

'I want to write too. Poetry I think. And maybe short stories.' Norris turned to me and put down the jar. 'Do you think that's silly? Dad says I'll never make any money.' He frowned at the bee, which was slowly raising and lowering its wings.

'Depends what you want. I'll come to your book launches if I'm not too busy editing my magazine.'

'Sure,' said Norris, nodding his head. His pale red hair flopped around his face like the ears of a friendly dog.

We sat and silently contemplated our futures.

'I heard you've got a tattoo,' he said eventually.

I felt myself flush as I lifted the right leg of my shorts to reveal the little black and yellow Smiley Face.

'I wanted something classic, but not a heart or a bluebird.'

'It's cute,' he said, stroking it lightly. 'Did it hurt?'

'Not really,' I said, mesmerized by his touch and the way our faces suddenly came together. All the tastes – salt, bitter, sweet and sour – were in his mouth. When our lips finally parted company we looked for the bee, but the syrup had worked its magic.

Halfway through the summer a heat wave struck. Water tanks ran dry and holidaymakers began leaving the beach in droves. Houses and baches sat empty. For Sale and Rent signs sprang up like desert flowers on their arid front lawns.

Norris and I met every afternoon. He'd wait on the corner of my street and I would walk towards him as casually as I could, my whole being pushing through the distance between us in which the air seemed as thick as jelly.

'You look nice,' he'd say. 'Have you done something to your hair?'

'No, not really,' I'd lie, wondering if my mother had noticed her bottle of expensive conditioning treatment was nearly empty.

We bought milkshakes and sat in the park under the pohutukawa trees. The cool sweetness flavoured our mouths with lime and strawberry as we took turns with each other's straws. The needles of pohutukawa flowers drifted down, making a crimson carpet.

'Come on,' said Norris, getting up and holding out his hand. 'I want to show you something.'

We climbed the hill behind the dunes, the sun pumping down on our backs. Norris led me to the shallow crater of what must have been a small extinct volcano, lined with kikuyu grass.

'Lie down, like this, and shut your eyes,' said Norris, wriggling into position, his head over the edge of the curve. Mystified, I did as he said.

'Now tip your head back and look.'

Earth and sky flipped over. Cupped by the arc of the green rim, the intense blue of the sky was transformed into a celestial dome. A huge, all-seeing eye. We were holding hands on the edge of the cosmos.

I asked Norris how he'd discovered the amazing way the crater re-shaped the sky.

'I came up here last summer and lay down for a rest. I fell asleep, and when I woke up I stretched and pushed my head over the rim. I couldn't believe it. It was like looking into God's eye.'

'Have you shown anyone else?' I asked.

'Only you,' he said, smiling his slow smile.

Three days later we lay on the floor of the empty bach we'd broken into, using our damp, sandy beach towels as blankets. Sunlight sneaked through the gaps in the tightly shut venetian blinds, falling on our scattered clothes. I was curled around Norris with one hand on his damp chest, the other numb beneath my side, not wanting to move. We dozed until we heard a car pull up outside.

A key scraped the lock of the front door. Voices came closer as we jumped to our feet, clutching our clothes to our bodies as we struggled into them on our way to the unlocked back door. We ran down to the beach and collapsed onto the sand, me on top of him.

'I love you,' I said, the words tumbling out of my mouth like loaded dice, before I could stop them.

'I've never known anyone like you, Ally,' said Norris, stroking my hair.

'What do you mean?' I asked, a cloud passing over the sun and a chill creeping over me.

'You're different from other girls. So direct. Intense. Not like the ones my mother's always trying to set me up with. Maybe I should tell her about you.'

The next day I arrived first at the empty bach we'd agreed to meet at. I scrambled in through the open laundry window and waited in the airless, empty front room, anxiously glancing out through the grubby net curtains. I counted the dead flies on the windowsill. There were nine altogether. I sighed and their desiccated, iridescent bodies drifted off the sill in a final flight. I studied the white stripe of skin where my watch used to be before I'd left it in the dunes. I wondered about putting a fake tan on, to blend it in. I had a flash of guilt about whether Grandad, who'd given the watch to me for my birthday, had noticed its absence. After about an hour I walked home along the beach, half blinded by hot tears.

I didn't see Norris again. I went around to his house one night but it was empty. Heavy curtains were drawn over the windows like shrouds. For the first time I noticed how much bigger and more expensive looking it was compared to ours, its paintwork fresh and garden manicured.

I stayed inside for the rest of the holidays. The door that Norris had opened inside me had slammed shut. I lay on my bed listening to the songs we'd heard, over and over again. Sifting through every conversation we'd had, looking for clues. My body coiling up like a spring every time the phone rang. The last weeks of summer dragged by like an unwilling dog, choking on an ever-tightening leash of heat.

I wondered if Norris knew he'd turned my world upside down, literally and metaphysically. Nothing ever looked quite the same again. I licked my lips, searching for that almost-forgotten combination of tastes: salt, bitter, sweet and sour.

I closed the book and took it to the counter.

Peace in our Time

Kevin Ireland

'Forgetting is the entrance-way to the new order – who wrote that?' Chenks asked. 'Or did anybody? Is it a quote from somewhere?'

'I'm afraid I must have forgotten,' said Etty, raising her voice so that she could be heard clearly from the bedroom. 'Which makes me a prime candidate, I suppose. For the new order, I mean.'

Chenks took a while to reply, then he said in his most relaxed yet confident courtroom manner, 'Only if you could prove you really did know in the first place. Otherwise not. You wouldn't qualify if you merely thought you'd forgotten. Not according to the formula as written.'

'Hold on a minute,' Etty replied. 'What happens if you really did know once, but you've forgotten you've forgotten, and everyone else has forgotten too? You wouldn't know you'd ever known, would you? Nobody would. And that means there couldn't be any conclusive test for getting in, could there? So where's your new order then? Am I being logical?'

This time Chenks grunted, but didn't answer, so Etty walked through to the lounge and found him stretched out on the sofa reading a paperback.

He had started his holiday before her.

'I might've known,' she said. 'You're into the holiday books already. Would you like a coffee?'

'Affirmative,' he replied without looking up.

'Well, I'm still doing the chores, so what about getting off your fat posterior and making me one too.'

Chenks lowered the book and gazed at his wife. 'That was a trick question. If you wanted coffee you only had to ask.'

'Come on darling. I've made your bed as well as mine, so you fix the coffee. That's reasonable.'

'My posterior is not fat,' Chenks complained, getting up and slinging the book aside. 'It's in perfect proportion to the rest of my body.'

'You're overweight and you know it,' said Etty. 'I keep telling you to drink your coffee black. Everyone in Russell will laugh at you.'

With a groan Chenks went to the fridge and opened the door. 'There's no bloody milk in any case,' he announced. 'There was milk in here half an hour ago. Where's it gone?'

'I've just thrown it out. You know very well how milk stinks when it goes off, don't you?'

There was no safe answer to that. The last time they'd gone on holiday Chenks had managed to leave a carton open on the kitchen table and after a week away the stench had been sickening.

He made black coffee for two, then looked at his watch and said, 'Let's drink this up and go. I'd rather set off now than read any more of that book.'

'What's it called?' Etty asked.

'Something stupid,' Chenks answered vaguely. The title had puzzled him, which is why he'd picked it out from their holiday paperbacks.

Etty walked to the sofa, turned the book over and glanced at the cover. '*Sex and the Mid-Life Crisis: A Guide for Absentminded Lovers*,' she read. 'Yucky.'

'I told you it's stupid. I'm certainly not taking it with us.'

'I should hope not. They'll think we're perverts.'

'Who will?'

'Everybody. The hotel guests. People on the beach. The chambermaids.'

Etty rinsed out their coffee cups and left them in the sink. Chenks watched her for a few moments, decided against advising her to wash them properly, then picked up their bags, went to the door and made straight for the car while Etty had a last look around to make sure that all the appliances except the refrigerator and deep-freeze were turned off and the whole place was locked up tight.

'By the way, I think you'll find they're not called chambermaids any more,' he said flippantly, when she'd finished her security check and was sitting beside him in the front of the car. 'In fact, you could risk the wrath of the Human Rights Commission for referring to a girl – sorry, I mean young woman – as a chambermaid. Come to think of it, I don't have a clue what they call them nowadays, do you? Certainly it wouldn't be anything connected with either chambers or maids. Something fancy and confusing, like accommodation supervisors, I expect.'

'They're still chambermaids to me,' Etty insisted.

'Anyway,' she went on, as they negotiated the first corner at the end of their road and she had gone through her departure drill one last time, trying to remember whether she really had checked all the windows and made sure the burglar alarm was on. 'Tell me more about the book. The one you were reading. What's its line? Dirty stuff, or just some kind of manual?'

'I'd place it in the high-minded but decidedly unhelpful category. I came across it in that heap of paperbacks Anna gave you.'

'Anna? Why would she give me a book like that?'

Chenks shrugged and hoped Etty would let the matter drop. There was something quite peculiar about the title. 'Did you remember to bring that bottle of gin?' he asked.

'I packed it last night. You watched me. Have you forgotten already?' she answered. Then after a short pause she said, 'It's not as if it's her kind of thing. The book, I mean. Anna's far too young for that sort of crisis. And surely she doesn't think we look as though we need help. I simply can't imagine why she'd buy it in the first place, let alone shove it in with a pile of light reading for the beach. It doesn't make sense. What have you been saying to her?'

Chenks adjusted the rear-vision mirror, as if that might help him think backwards. He couldn't see how the damned book could possibly have any relevance to him. However, he answered carefully, 'Nothing.'

'Are you sure?'

'I swear it. Nothing.'

Etty gazed thoughtfully at Chenks. Cross-examination was his bread and butter, so how come he was looking so uncomfortable? Why was he so solemn? Why was he fidgeting with the mirror and taking such a long time to answer? She settled back and consoled herself with the reflection that you only had to ask men a question connected in some remote way with sex and they immediately became shifty. Men were hopelessly imprecise about their relationships. That was one of the big differences.

To Chenks's relief, Etty stopped probing him about the book and he managed to forget about it entirely – until she brought the subject up again late that same afternoon.

They had arrived at their hotel by the beach and they had immediately blobbed out on the sand, reading and swimming. Then they had taken a hot shower, while they thought about going out to eat, and they were sitting in their room wrapped only in towels.

Chenks opened the bottle of the gin and he was topping up their glasses with one of the large bottles of tonic they'd also been clever enough to bring – it was going to save them heaps over the mini-bar prices, not because he was poor or mean, but as a matter of principle – when Etty said, without prior warning, 'I still can't get over Anna smuggling in that tacky little item on sex among the Sara Paretskys, can you? I simply can't believe it wasn't deliberate. I'm glad I caught you reading it. I would've been most upset to find we'd brought it with us.'

'You didn't *catch me* doing anything,' Chenks protested. Then he decided that he was being far too defensive. In such situations the best policy was always to mount a light counterattack.

'I saw the silly thing for the first time this morning while I was waiting for you to finish all those chores that didn't really need doing,' he said. 'The title popped out and hit me in the eye, just as the publishers intended. If you cast your mind back you may be able to recollect that I drew your attention to it. I even asked you a question.'

'Yes, so you did, Chenky darling. That's quite right, I remember now,' Etty agreed, stirring her drink with a finger. 'By the way, this gin's far too stiff. Do you want to see me collapse into my dinner plate in front of everyone?'

Chenks got up and splashed more tonic into both their glasses. As he did so, his towel came undone and fell to the carpet. Etty stared at her husband as he stood there naked, a thing she would never have done at home, but somehow it was different when you were in the far north, among all the other holidaymakers.

'Do you remember what the question was?' she asked, sucking the gin off her finger.

'What question?'

'The one you asked me this morning. The one to do with the book.'

'It was something about forgetting,' Chenks said patiently. 'I seem to remember there was a whole chapter on the processes of forgetting. Everything from Alzheimer's to…' He paused and laughed. 'I've completely forgotten…'

Etty giggled, drained her glass and, as she got dressed to go out, allowed herself to be persuaded that they ought to have a second generous gin to balance the first, on the sensible grounds that no one ever saw a bird fly on one wing.

They were quite light headed when they began their meal, but they had no trouble sinking a bottle of chardonnay, so when they had finished Chenks suggested a sobering walk along the beach and back.

Gazing at the moon on the sea and the silhouettes of the trees as they strolled along the sand would have made the perfect end to the day, if they hadn't discovered as soon as they returned to the hotel that the walk had made them thirsty again. This meant a detour to a bar where Chenks decided that, because they'd saved so much on gin, they were absolutely entitled to lash out on a rather good cognac.

By the time they arrived in their room again it was quite late, they were in an exalted mood and they simply chucked off their clothes and made love energetically in the larger of their two beds.

It must have been at about two in the morning that Chenks woke with a start. It took some time for him to realise that he was lying beside his wife in a hotel bedroom with a view of the bay, for he had been having a horrifying dream about Anna.

Then he discovered that he had become tangled in the top sheet of the bed and by the time he had unwound it from his arms and legs he was left with only an obscure and unsettling notion of how Anna had been threatening him. The details of the dream had slipped away.

He got up, poured a glass of cold tonic water, then looked down at his wife in the dim, grey light that filtered through their room through French doors that she had recklessly asked him to leave open to allow the cool night breeze to enter.

The way Etty was stretched out naked across the bed made her look as though she was posing for one of those misty, erotic illustrations Chenks had seen in arty magazines. Her hair streamed across a pillow, caught in the swirl of an invisible current, and she held one arm in front of her as if to clutch hold of him and draw him down into the depths beside her. She was no longer the Etty he knew, the practical, hard-working, managerial Etty of the everyday world. She had become bewitching and mysterious – a nereid, Chenks thought, submerged in her perfect liquid element. All his wrestling and kicking to unwind himself from the top sheet hadn't disturbed her sleep in the slightest. She hadn't even stirred or groaned.

Chenks gazed at his wife in admiration for several minutes, then it struck him that it must have been a year ago, on Vanuatu, that he had last taken time off to surrender to visual pleasure like this. Etty and he simply didn't go in for this kind of thing. Not only weren't they the sentimental type, but they were surrounded by impediments. Twin beds, pyjamas, busy professional lives and a well-organised domestic routine, all conspired to separate their existences. Holidays in hotels, once a year, provided their only opportunity to indulge themselves in each other. It was strange, when he thought about it. They lived together in close proximity, yet scarcely ever checked out what they really looked like in the flesh.

After refilling his glass, Chenks went to the doors. There was enough room outside for two chairs and a table. Quietly, he pushed the chairs sideways, then he sat on one and put his feet up on the other, so that he gazed directly over the sands to the silver sea. He thought again of Etty lying there, looking so attractive, so devastating, then he remembered making love. It had been like… Well, why not admit it? It had been as exciting as making love with a complete stranger. He wondered if Etty had known that feeling, too.

Damn Anna, he thought. She had very nearly spoilt their arrival.

That book really had been a premeditated piece of mischief. But what was her motive? And why had she now intruded into his dream? What harm had he done her? It wasn't as if he could remember making a pass at her or anything gross like that.

Then piece by piece he began to construct a likely answer. He thought back to a party that Etty and he had thrown just before Easter. It was the last time Anna had spent the whole evening with them.

The silly woman had arrived with her latest conquest, which was perfectly all right so far as he was concerned, except that this one happened to be some hunk from the gym she went to. He must have been a good fifteen years younger than her. The way she had flounced around had been almost offensive. He had felt compelled to do something about it.

So, all right, what if he had spoilt her fun a bit by asking her pointedly, in front of the hunk and several assorted friends, how Charlie-boy was getting along in his lush, new pastures. What a conversation stopper that had been. A direct hit. Just a few simple words – which, after all, happened to be the way he earned his living – and he'd caught her fair and square. Served her right for making such a fool of herself. Charles may have been a major mistake, but that didn't mean she could behave as if he had never happened. Some people had longer memories than she might care to be reminded of.

Chenks got up and stretched, then shut the doors and padded back across the room to bed. He felt better now that he had sorted out what Anna was up to. It had to be a simple matter of revenge. Well, she would learn. Any more tricks and next time he'd really fix her.

For the rest of the night Chenks had perfect rest and in the morning he woke in what he told Etty was 'a sublime holiday mood'. There were no more tangled sheets and the little nightmare he'd experienced had been entirely overlaid by a second vivid dream in which he and his wife were swimming naked through a summer sky, in and out of fluffy little clouds, drinking enormous glasses of cognac.

It was exasperating, then, to have to sit through breakfast while Etty still banged on about the book. 'I wonder what she thinks she's up to,' Etty said. 'That subtitle. The *Absentminded Lovers* bit. She's hatching some sort of plot, isn't she?'

'Anna? A plot? I'd love to think so. But she's not that complicated. It's just a coincidence. She sorts out a pile of books, and that one gets mixed up with the others – end of story.'

'Rubbish,' Etty insisted. 'It's part of a message. I'm not naïve, you know, whatever you may think.'

Chenks managed to control himself and say quietly, 'Forget it, will you darling. You're the least naïve person I've ever met, so I simply can't understand why it's bothering you. It could just as easily have been some dog-eared paperback on the ancient Etruscans. Anna isn't that devious.'

'Yes she is,' Etty maintained. 'I'm her oldest friend, apart from you, and I'd say devious just about sums her up – when she's in one of her moods. Which happens every so often.'

'Hmm,' said Chenks and let the matter drop.

To his immense relief, no further mention was made of *Sex and the Mid-Life Crisis* for the next two days, and he had managed to shove the whole subject to the back of his mind, when Etty made a remark over a late afternoon gin that made him nearly spill his drink.

'Anna's always been sweet on you, did you know that?' Etty asked, right out of the blue – which was no idle cliché, for they were sitting outside their room, beneath a cloudless sky, which only a few moments previously Etty had said looked as though their attractive but grumpy chambermaid had scrubbed it, then pegged it out across the dome of heaven to dry, a remark that Chenks thought as unlikely as it was perfectly poetic.

'*Sweet?*' he repeated. 'What makes you use a silly word like that?'

'Well?' Etty demanded.

'Well what?'

'Well, what are you going to do about it? With Anna? I have a right to know.'

'For God's sake, Etty, stop talking such garbage. Anna's not only not sweet, she's gone decidedly sour on me for some reason.'

'Don't try that line on me. Women can tell these things. The pair of you have been discussing some kind of unfinished business and that book was part of the conversation. It all fits.'

The gin tasted marvellous. How come, Chenks asked himself, it was never like this at home? It was the perfect holiday drink, yet he couldn't face it in any other circumstance. In fact, he would go a long way to avoid gin in Auckland.

He turned the drink around in his hand, then held it up to the sky, developing its hint of steely greyness into a full rich blue. Slowly he allowed himself to relax, then he said steadily, 'I don't know what's eating you, Etty dear. But let me spell this out once and for all – Anna and I have always known each other well, but that's as far as it has ever gone. We have never been what you might call intimate. And that's the way I intend to keep it, and I'm sure I speak for her too. Does that satisfy you?'

'She introduced us. Remember?'

'You're being a little forgetful, dear. As I recollect the event, we had already spoken, then all she did was chip in later and ask if we'd met. That's not what I'd call an introduction. We didn't need her help.'

'How very interesting,' Etty said. 'I wish we'd talked about this before, because there's something you've neglected to mention.'

'What's that?'

'When you and I first got together, Anna whipped straight in to tell me to keep off her patch. She had long-term plans for you – and you knew it.'

Chenks laughed, though not happily. 'She wouldn't have said those things. She wouldn't have used phrases like keeping off her patch or having plans for people.'

'*Absentminded Lovers*,' Etty said sharply. 'She's got a point you know. You've forgotten all about your exact relationship at the time, haven't you? You've even forgotten how she used to speak. And now, for some reason, she's reminding you about it. I don't think you're telling me the truth, do you know that, Mr Raymond Chenkley?'

'Listen, *Mrs* Antoinette Chenkley,' her husband responded. 'I need another gin. A large one. And I would advise you to have one too. If you're spoiling for a fight, you may as well be able to blame the booze when you recover later.'

'Chenky darling,' Etty said. 'Don't get all shirty with me. And, yes, I'm just in the mood for another gin. How the hell Eugene Onegin got by on a single shot I'll never know. Perhaps he took it straight from the bottle.'

In spite of his anger, Chenky had to smile. The thing he liked about Etty was that despite being highly strung and obsessive, and despite being cursed with a nit-picking memory for precisely the kind of things he preferred to forget, she could sometimes be so beautifully dotty that she caught you right off balance. He stepped back into their room to collect the ingredients he had stashed in the mini-bar, then he refilled their glasses and told himself to keep his temper and try to see the funny side.

'Let's call a truce on the book, shall we?' he asked when he returned. 'I'm absolutely fed up with it as a topic of conversation. And if it really was intended as a weapon of some sort, I would suggest that our best strategy is to ignore it. So, no more talk about absentminded lovers for the rest of the week, okay?'

Etty looked at her husband shrewdly, then she fished a tiny lump of ice from her drink and rolled it around her tongue. 'Why do they always make midget ice cubes in these places?' she asked, mumbling a little. 'Why don't they make proper-sized lumps? I mean, why the frugality? What are they saving?'

'Truce?' Chenks asked again.

'I'm not talking about it any more, am I?'

'Pax? Peace in our time? No more mention of nasty books?'

'Pax.' Etty agreed, swallowing the last fragment of ice. 'But I'm going straight around to Anna's when we get back, to tell her I enjoyed her little joke. She won't get away with it.'

'Tell her what you like,' Chenks said. 'Just as long as peace prevails within these four walls all the time we are here.'

Etty blew her husband a kiss. What idiots men were, she thought. So inconsistent, so imprecise when it came to the fierce complexities of the heart. They were so dozy, so unaware of danger. They didn't have a clue how to save themselves when deadly little words swept them out of their depth. They just blustered and floundered about, splashed, shouted for help – then forgot what they were doing and under they went.

And for the rest of Chenks's stay that should have been the end of the whole business about the book – if something quite unpredictable had not happened.

One of Chenks's great professional strengths was that he possessed what he called his automatic crap-detector, which always set off alarm bells when he was in danger of being lulled into a smug sense of security, so when he now fell victim to a moment of summer madness it seemed to him afterwards as though only Anna could have been to blame. She had somehow managed to make him feel that he had triumphed over her in the silly matter of the book, while all the time she had been neutralising his defences. Perhaps she had even enlisted the Devil himself to whisper in his ear.

It was on the last day of the holiday and he had the glorious prospect of a couple of hours alone in which to savour a final buzz of holiday euphoria. For the first time in almost twelve months he felt cut free from the person he had moulded himself into and, instead, he had become a man designed by nature to focus his existence on drinking gin, making love to a strange and beautiful woman, and gazing at night from a bedroom at a glittering strip of sand and sea.

When he tried to imagine being back in Auckland, wearing a suit and tie, behaving like one of the pillars of the community (which, after all, he was), relying on a secretary to organise his life, making courtroom speeches, earning good money, wearing pyjamas and sleeping alone, he seemed to be inventing the mid-life predicament of an especially forgetful alien. These were fictions, they were not the habits of a man in the prime of his life who was born to be a beachcomber.

Absent-mindedly he strolled down towards the sea. Etty had told him that she had some last-minute shopping to do at the boutique shopping centre near the hotel – there were small presents to be bought, plus a whole lot of brilliant new bathing suits that she needed to take a long look at, though why she should want to do so at the end of the holiday rather than the beginning was a mystery that he knew to be beyond all human understanding. So when she had said she'd see him at the beach later, he calculated from experience that this meant she would turn up just in time to collect him for lunch.

Chenks slipped off his shirt and packed it into the beach bag he carried on his shoulder. In a broad-brimmed straw hat and with his towel wrapped around his swimming togs, he felt he cut an impressive figure. He wasn't really overweight, just well-rounded, and he had been careful only to expose himself to the beginning of a pleasant tan.

In fact, Chenks felt so completely at ease that he stopped and bought a Coke, a drink which, like gin, he would never have held in his hand in Auckland from one year's end to the next. He sat for a while, sipping from the can, then sauntered slowly down to the beach.

Etty and he had made a habit of spreading themselves out just beyond a thick clump of trees at the far end of the beach, well away from the crowd, and they had come to think of it as their own private property, a territory that no one else was entitled to. They considered the occasional passers-by to be trespassers and either ignored them to make them feel unwelcome or glared at them until they took the hint and went back to join the fun-makers. So for one last nostalgic time he headed towards their secluded domain.

But as soon as he stepped past the trees he saw a woman stretched out on the very spot that Etty and he had made their own. He stopped and stared. The last thing he had expected at such a significant private moment was an interloper. Why wasn't she chirping and lolling about and oiling herself among the other frantic holiday-makers where she belonged? Why was she deliberately trying to wreck his final romantic impressions?

For a minute he thought of giving up and walking back to the hotel. Then he silently asked himself a strange spur-of-the-moment question: 'How could I be so sure that fate has intervened to mess things up? Looked at any other way, perhaps someone else in my position would think that this was, indeed, the final romantic impression he had been seeking. A kind of gift – a farewell memento – from the sea.'

Chenks looked around carefully. Etty was nowhere in sight. Well, he thought to himself, I've been blamed for doing far worse with Anna, so why not talk to the woman? The situation had amusing possibilities, and there was absolutely no possibility of danger. After all, he had already packed up and he would disappear shortly, possibly forever. There wasn't even time to buy the woman a drink. There would just be a brief conversation, then a moment of parting, followed by a heart-wrenching feeling of what might have been. Nothing serious would happen and no one would be any the wiser.

In fact, the more he thought about it, the more intriguing the whole situation seemed. So how to begin?

Chenks approached, threw down his straw hat, dropped the beach bag from his shoulder, then knelt on the sand near the woman. Her head was turned away from him and was hidden under a towel which, exactly like her bathing suit, was chocolate brown and covered with a striking pattern of white palm trees.

Again Chenks gazed around to make sure that his wife was not approaching.

So, what should he say?

Best undoubtedly to stick to a holiday theme.

He cleared his throat huskily.

'Are you enjoying the sun?' he asked.

The head shook itself slightly beneath the towel.

'Huh?' it said.

Oh no, Chenks thought, what if she turns out to be grumpy, like the chambermaid? What if it *is* the chambermaid?

Simply cut and run, he told himself, that would be the best policy.

'Are you enjoying the sun?' he asked again.

The woman became very still, then again she replied, 'Huh?', though this time with a definite rise in tone.

'Have you just arrived? I don't think I've seen you on the beach before. I'm sure I would have noticed someone with a figure like yours,' he went on. He knew the words were banal, but he was sure he was uttering them in confident, man-of-the-world tones.

The woman pushed herself up on one elbow and tugged the towel away from her face. She was furious. 'What the hell do you think you're playing at?' Etty said. 'Trying to pick up your own wife?'

'Listen, Etty…' Chenks said stupidly, for he couldn't think of anything else to add.

'Listen? *Listen?*' she screamed. 'That's the filthiest thing you've ever done...' Then she looked down at her towel and bathing suit and almost spat at him, 'Seven years of marriage and I'm still a stranger – you couldn't recognise me in my new... You dirty old goat... Oh, damn you Chenky, that's the most insulting...'

She was still shouting at him as he got up and walked towards the sea – rattling on about how she'd gone to all the trouble to rush in to buy the expensive bathing suit and towel set she had longed for all week, then coming straight down here to wait for him as a surprise. But Chenks was only half-listening. The important thing was to come up with an answer that would be good enough to hold up as an impregnable defence through the years to come.

Then he had it. The obvious solution was to pass the whole thing off as a prank. Over his shoulder he yelled at her, 'Oh, for crying out loud, Etty, can't you tell when someone's pulling your leg? Can't you take a bloody joke?'

He would work on it later, refining the words and polishing his excuse into a really bold piece of tom-foolery. He would have to make her laugh. But just for now, while Etty was in such a stinking temper, the sensible thing would be to keep a safe distance. He entered the water, stepped quickly to meet the first small wave that rippled towards him, leapt over it, then crashed with an immense splash into the sea. It was delicious. He wiped his eyes and rolled over on his back.

Well, that beats everything, Chenks told himself. To think how all that worry about a single little book could entice a man to behave in a way that was so dumb, so completely out of character. For that had to be the explanation – the book and Anna were responsible. It wasn't his fault. The whole fiasco had been devised like a time-bomb to make a complete mess of their holiday. Anna had programmed everything right from the beginning. All that mid-age crises and forgetful lover business.

He might have realised right from the very start that Etty was right. Anna had been out to set a sophisticated, elegant and thoroughly vicious, little booby-trap.

Chenks kicked his legs frog-like against the water and looked up into the sky. There was not a cloud in sight. Perhaps, he considered, he should take the sky to be an omen that everything would be all right, that in next to no time he would be able to walk from the sea again, laughing in satisfaction at the way he'd tricked his wife. Etty – it would soon turn out – had been hoodwinked completely. It would be ludicrous for anyone to think that he was incapable of recognising his own wife. She would soon share his triumph. She would giggle with pleasure at his mastery of the art of the practical joke.

In quite another part of his thoughts, however, he was also beginning to deal seriously with the question of Anna and the book. He remembered a conversation he'd had with somebody, somewhere, sometime, just before he had left to come on holiday. The phrase that seemed somehow to have stuck in his mind was something to do with forgetting you'd forgotten.

Now, there was a real problem, wasn't there? What was it between Anna and himself that he couldn't now remember ever remembering?

Surely, he told himself optimistically, it couldn't have been very important if he'd forgotten it. He hoped Etty's splendid, poetic, off-beat sense of humour wouldn't desert her in the days to come.

Where We Floated the Pohutukawa Wreath

Kath Beattie

Barefoot and three abreast we trail the shallows, a warm zephyr puffing strands of hair, iridescent pebbles tumbling, pink crabs scuttling as the Pacific tide stretches fingers toward the bush and farmland. Morton Bay, and we're here on the annual pilgrimage pondering the mystery of the magnetism.

This time I have vowed to confess. I will tell the other two the simple truth, the real reason I need to return again and again.

As they lose steam elaborating the serenity and fulfillment of their souls it's my turn. 'I come,' I blurt, fingering the mother-of-pearl penknife I wear as a pendant, my voice thin in the salt air, 'to resolve my guilt over Barney.'

The backwash swishes broken paua and tuatua shells across our toes and we stop and turn to one another. Angie breaks the spell. 'Guilt? What guilt? He's not dead! I saw him last week.'

I'd swear in a court of law (and I work there now as the judge's clerk) that the lazy wave curling up and up ready to tip and race, holds fast at the peak of its turn, remains frozen as if I've taken a photo. My breath follows suit and I glimpse Amy's tonsils through her gaping mouth and think, she's been sucking pink pencils.

'I knew you'd both freak,' Angie says. 'He was in a wine bar in Auckland.'

'Auckland!' Amy's voice runs a C minor scale. 'He can't be, he's down there!' She arcs a finger at the sea bed in the middle of the bay.

Angie tosses her auburn curls (I say 'her' as we are an identical trio and Amy and I remain 'original' streaky-mouse). 'I never in a million years believed he drowned.'

'Angie! It was you who wailed until Dad relented and rowed us to the spot where we floated a pohutukawa wreath.'

Angie plinks a pebble into the waves. 'For heavens sake! That was years ago ... emotions at ten or eleven or whatever I was ... (Amy and I overlay Angie's 'I' with 'we') ... and I've had time to ...'

'Review the situation?' Amy and I chime together, imitating one of Angie's stock phrases she uses as a police detective.

'Yes ... well ... I certainly did after I saw him.'

'Or thought you did.'

'It *was* him. I'd know him anywhere.'

Morton Bay, Christmas holidays and Barney Lucas are as intertwined as we triplets. Amy reckons that our parents should have adopted Barney, then what finally happened wouldn't have. Angie says 'Rot. Barney was a loner. He didn't want nor need a family and anyway Aurora (that's me) wouldn't have let him use her bedroom all year.'

'True.' It was okay sharing the double bed with the other two for a few weeks. But all year? Every year? First of all Angie has this way of referring to me as if I'm not present. All our lives (and we're forty-something now and 'going backwards') Angie still speaks as if I'm on another planet. It drives me bananas. We'd be tucked under the duvet, Angie's elbow splintering my ribs, her high pitched whine splitting the darkness. 'Get Aurora's feet off me,' or, 'Why doesn't Aurora sleep with her head down the bottom?'

Barney referred to us as the 'trio' but reckoned Angie would have been happier as a single. My thoughts exactly.

Barney lived at the Children's Home on the north coast and prior to each school holiday Mum phoned the matron and a week later Barney arrived on the cream launch.

We'd balance on the veranda railings and watch for the first glint of sun on the twin-screw windshield as it laboured around Horseshoe Point at the head of the bay and nosed its way into our jetty. 'He's here!' we'd yell and leg it across the paddock and stream to meet him. 'Hi trio,' he'd call and ruffle our hair or punch us on the upper arms.

Barney was five years older than us. The first time we met he was ten and knew how to do reef knots and string tricks and we taught him how to hand-milk 'Jersey-Girl' and ride woolly wethers. He arrived with a beaten-up bag he called a hold-all. Angie said, 'It doesn't look like it holds much to me,' and Barney replied, 'That's because I have my skin and wits and don't need much else.' Mum later took we three aside and told us to be careful what we said as 'orphaned children are poor wee things and it would be wrong to make a show of what we had.' I couldn't help thinking that Barney had quite a lot. Cigarettes for one. Not even Dad could afford those. 'Bad for your lungs,' he said. But then Dad's excuse for anything he couldn't or wouldn't afford came into the 'bad for you' category: icing sugar, new curtains, coloured pencils for school.

I asked Barney how new curtains could be 'bad for you' and he said they had chemicals all over them that rotted your brain. And coloured pencils? 'Well,' he expounded, 'little squirts like you suck the ends, your gut gets to look like a rainbow then your pee turns red or green or whatever pencil you're sucking.' I've never been able to put one in my mouth since, though Amy was skeptical and asked later when we lay hot and stuck together in the double bed what colour wees you got if you sucked all the pencils one after the other. Angie said, 'Aurora's would be striped.'

Angie now denies she ever said that and addresses me directly rather than through Amy. 'You, Aurora have never changed. Because you're three minutes older, you think you have the cap on all knowledge and I'm telling you now that I saw him. He is so unique I could not be mistaken.'

'You've got a nose like a parrot,' I said to him when he first came and was given a Chinese burn for my rudeness. Later in bed we three added further observations. Lollipop hair, freckled legs that looked like camouflage, and the mysterious colour of his eyes. We argued about it for weeks. Still do.

'It was the eyes.' Angie pauses for our reaction. 'Navy-blue. Dark navy-blue.'

Amy spooks her voice. 'Indigo, the colour of conger eels.'

'Purple,' I state with my eldest triplets' 'don't mess with me' tone that Angie hates so much. 'As purple as the shadow on the headland,' and I point.

As the one who claims to have seen him, Angie has the last say. 'There can't be anyone else in the world with eyes of such intense fathomless navy-blue.'

Amy pops a seaweed bead with her toe. 'Except maybe ... his parents.' In the silence a gull calls, a haunting cry that turns our gaze out to sea. She pops another bead. 'And they're dead or in Peru or Belize or somewhere.'

Angie's chin sharpens. 'You didn't believe all that did you?'

Before the happening we believed everything Barney told us. He was the nearest thing we had to an encyclopaedia.

Fire originated from dragon's breath, touch an electric fence and you died before sunset, dogs turned to wolves when the moon came out ...

His knowledge rivaled the Bible. And he had information about that too, some of it in rhyme. Repeating it made Hell seemed closer than the front gate. Dad and Mum wore Christian glasses and were full of praises.

'Such a helpful young fellow, willing to join in, take his share of chores, kind to the girls...' We, the 'trio' had a more comprehensive view. Never let him hold a frog, never climb a tree ahead of him, never play 'shut-your-eyes-and-open-your-mouth' games.

'How come you're an orphan?' Amy once asked. We were building a castle at the half tide mark where we could capture waves for the moat. Angie dropped the rock she was carrying for the dam, sending a flood over our legs. 'Amy! We're not allowed ...'

Barney tapped the side of his nose. 'Promise not to tell?'

The moat forgotten, we sat cross-legged on the crusty sand while Barney disclosed that he was not an orphan but the son of fugitives. His parents had robbed a bank and escaped to Fiji, then Peru. 'Every pig in New Zealand is looking for them.' (I imagined hundreds of porkers rooting New Zealand to smithereens.) 'There's a reward of three million pastas if you find them.'

'Pastas?'

'Peru money, dummy!'

With the nucleus of the skeptic's nose even then, Angie asked, 'How?'

'How what?'

'Did they do the robbery?'

The tunnel of crime took weeks and almost as long to tell. It involved mole-like burrowings under the main street and building, many collapses and much more careful ditching of the excess dirt behind their own home. It meant carrying jack hammers and jemmies (tools we'd never heard of) and .303s (which we had). It involved stealing a van and a yacht. 'A ketch I expect,' Amy intervened. 'They're best in the ocean.' (As coastal dwellers we were up on such matters.)

'That's it kid! I knew it had a 'ch' in it. 'Albatross' it was called.'

Angie stared Barney down. 'Albatrosses are bad luck.'

Barney hung a forlorn head. 'Maybe that's why they've never come back for me. They promised they would.'

'What about the money,' Angie persisted. 'You can't use our money in Fiji.'

Superiority lit Barney's face. 'It's laundered, silly! And becomes whatever dosh you want.'

We three mulled the story over as we lay in the double bed. Was it possible that our parents could abandon us as his had? Leave us in a Children's Home, never write or visit? Could the washing machine really change money? Next day Amy tried a ten cent piece she found in Dad's drawer. We never saw it again.

'Did you speak to him?'

We lean against a log swept in by the restless ocean, our faces turned toward the horizon, that lighter blue line where coastal ships once ploughed journeys that brought the outside world to us. Sometimes massive liners cruised past and we'd press our heads to the sand to hear the thud-thud-thud of engines and imagine rich Americans sitting on deck chairs, or we'd marvel at the arching rainbow spinnakers of sailing craft. The ocean brought us other bounty: buckets and ropes, a set of new towels still wrapped in plastic and once a crate of sodden books which we planned to dry and read but found they were scribed in Russian.

Angie writes her name in the sand with a driftwood stick. 'He knew me, no question! We caught each other's eyes. My mouth just opened in surprise, pronouncing "Barney!" Recognition flashed and as quickly disappeared ... as he did.'

'How's he got away with it Angie?' Amy's voice is tentative.

Angie shrugs.

'Come on! You're the detective ...'

Amy and I wait ... and wait. We're experienced at not hurrying Angie, she's always had that pedantic 'plod' sort of attitude. My mind returns to the excitement of an after-storm treasure hunt. Sometimes there were dead fish and crayfish pots, once a live sea horse left in a small rock pool. Amy's best find was a doll with a leg missing. She nursed her to good health (helped by a prosthesis courtesy of Dad). I am wondering what happened to 'Pegleg' when Angie says, 'Aurora will understand (she meant that I would as a 'court worker' but Amy wouldn't as a kindy teacher) that once a person is presumed dead then they just can't be brought back to life again. The most obvious is ...'

Amy interrupts (to ensure that 'kindy teachers' get some recognition for having brains), 'Yes! Yes! We get the drift. A new identity. But what about the parents? Did they pick him up? What's their story?'

Angie clamps lips and I make a sign for Amy to zip it for fear of Angie sulking for days. The silence drags and I eye sand-hoppers scuttling for safety as the tide creeps in. I can feel her bursting to tell and at the same time unwilling to give in until we beg, beg as we had to in the old days. *Oh come on Angie. Tell us. Out with it! You can have the first bath or the last sultana square or sleep with Pegleg.*

I can't believe that I still fall for her games, allow her to manipulate. I leap in. 'Let's short circuit this. They were crims, got arrested, jailed, escaped.'

Angie glares. 'There was only ever a mother. A lost soul no doubt. Never been located, probably dead by now and it's very unlikely that she made contact with Barney. He obviously staged the drowning, made for the bright lights. After all he was sixteen, wanting to leave the home, do his own thing. Don't you remember how he talked of adventuring ... travelling ... He'd have changed his name ... got a job ...'

Amy stands and thrusts a pointing arm. 'I don't believe a word of it.

Barney was a scallywag for sure but he would never want to burden us, hurt us, leave us forever wondering. He'd have shared his plans and sworn us to secrecy. For whatever reason he took the clinker, (her voice wavers) accidentally drowned and that's all there is to it. End of story.'

The night had been calm and moonlit. I woke to a thump on the verandah and a shadow passing the wide push-up window. The other two were comatose, Angie's arm flung across Amy who lay on her back. Why hadn't Dad woken? Why hadn't the dogs? I edged myself to a sitting position and leaned out. I glimpsed Barney caught in a patch of moonlight as he unlatched the gate. He was wearing his woolly hat with the wide white stripe, the one Mum knitted for his Christmas parcel. I slipped out the window and followed, darting from shadow to shadow until we reached the boat-shed. Barney dragged the clinker to the water, fetched the oars and placed them in the rowlocks before tiptoeing toward me in the shadow of the shed. Without a word he put his arms around me, squeezing till I had little breath, then kissed the top of my head and pressed his mother-of-pearl penknife into my hands. 'It's yours now,' he said and was gone. I waited a minute, listening to the slice of oars. A breeze ruffled my hair. 'Barney!' I called as I picked my way across mussel shells to the waters edge, 'the wind's rising.' Beyond the headland angry whitecaps would rear and spit and fight, retreat and clash again and again, consuming all that came in their way. The oars continued their dip and pull, moonlight flickered on the increasing swell and soon a velvet darkness engulfed. I stood clutching the penknife until my fingers and toes lost feeling, praying that he'd come back. My ears pricked when I thought I heard a thump and scrape but it could have been the sea rumbling and grumbling as it licked the land and swallowed whatever it wanted to.

I'd crept back and lain awake, my tummy churning, until Mum called us for breakfast. Dad burst in from the cowshed. 'Where's the lad?'

We all scouted around. 'The clinker's gone!' Angie yelled and Dad launched the old whaler and rowed back and forth across the bay, his face taut. Mum bailed and we stood on the shore sucking our fingers. They found the woolly hat bobbing on a current and brought it ashore as if it was Barney. In the afternoon we found the clinker smashed on the rocks, one oar tumbling back and forth in the crashing waves. No body was found.

Until now I have never told anyone of my stalking, not the family, not the police who came and searched the sea and shore and questioned Dad and Mum until they were almost ready to confess to anything, not the matron from the Children's Home. Not my husband nor my sons. I've been sure I was to blame. Why hadn't I woken my sisters, called my parents, made Barney come back. Why?

My sisters have no empathy with my guilt, their only interest is the penknife. It was Barney's only personal possession. They examine it, hold it to the light, open and shut the blades, caress the exquisite shell inlay. 'Touching it makes him seem close, real,' Amy says, clasping it to her chest, a tear trickling. 'He was so special. Better than a brother, more than a brother ...' Her eyes sparkle. 'And as I hold this I feel it's true, he is alive.'

Angie touches Amy's hand. 'I really really saw him.'

I see the glow on their faces. Feel it on my own. How could I not have realised? We each loved him separately but he loved us as one, 'the trio', an entity in itself. 'Others' behaved likewise. 'How are the triplets?' 'The threesome?' The penknife was not solely for me. It was Barney's gift to us, 'the triplets'. In the dark that night I was merely the 'trio' representative. 'You wear it,' I say to Amy. 'I've had it for too long.'

'We'll share,' she says.

We wander back toward the family homestead. Behind us the sea lullabies a constant song. At this time of evening holiday makers have retreated and the place is ours again. We hold hands and whoop and dance.

We're six or nine or fourteen. Just us and Morton Bay and the peace from knowing that Barney survived.

Hokianga

(Hoki, v.i. *return;* anga, n. *driving force, thing driven.*)

John MacKinven

Fiona doesn't often get back to the Hoke, but this summer she's taking her seventeen-year-old son Tom.

'What for?' If Tom had his way he'd never leave the city.

'To check out our old haunts,' Fiona says. 'Go blackberrying up the same dirt roads we did when you were little.'

'So what's in it for me?'

'Wait and see.' What can she say? Blackberries?

At least his bag is packed when it's time to leave. Promising, but he looks straight ahead as they drive and keeps his mouth shut. Fiona can hear the muffled poom-poom-poom of his iPod undercutting the drone of the motor. Never mind. She has memories to revisit and plans to make.

They stop for petrol where she used to put five bucks' worth at a time into the Morris Oxford ute. There's a proper shop front now and a forecourt rather than the two bowsers – one petrol, the other diesel – side-by-side on a gravelled mound. The workshop has been given a facelift, complete with a sliding door and an oil company logo.

Fiona turns off to drive up the valley and the road has dwindled to a track. The potholes need dodging and grass is showing between the wheel ruts. Past the one-way bridge, at the top of the uphill straight, Fiona comes face-to-face with the old house. There's a five-bar gate now but the paddock is full of ragwort in bloom. She drives on – knocking at the door is the last thing she'd do – and stops the car at the turnaround.

Time has diminished everything, even the hills, and rain is threatening. If the iPod was hers, 'A Woman's Heart' would top the playlist: My heart is low, so low…

'Could we just get to the beach, please?' Tom asks.

He's been dutiful so far and Fiona doesn't want to hang around either. They have a motel booked at Omapere. It's evening by the time they get there. Fiona gives the holiday mood one last try. 'Fish and chips?'

Opononi is five minutes away, and they eat in the car before crossing the road to the wharf. Daylight is fading. A brisk wind skims spray off the bar, bringing it on up the harbour. Fiona zips her jacket and turns her back on the sunset. Bravely, she asks, 'What do you think?'

'So this is the winterless north?' Sarcasm is second nature these days.

'What would you like to do tomorrow?' Braver still.

'Go back to Auckland.'

Fiona turns and walks to the car. They're here for the rest of the week and she's determined to make the most of it – even if that means leaving Tom in the motel unit all day, texting his discontent to his mates.

Tom was eighteen months old when his father was killed by a careless truckie. Mark had been down in Auckland looking for work when he was flipped off his motorbike on the Penrose interchange, and that was that.

Fiona went on a benefit and doubled her own unpaid secretarial workload for Friends of the Earth. It didn't just keep her busy. 'I need to go on reminding myself there's a world out there,' she told her friend Sophie. Hers was a number Fiona phoned often.

Sophie was green before it became a cause. They met at a public gathering in Rawene, convened to protect the harbour's mangroves, where Sophie spoke up about agricultural chemicals poisoning waterways and kai moana, about the damage to the sand dunes pine plantations were causing. 'I won't be giving up on this fight, girl. Not while I'm still breathing,' she said to Fiona afterwards. 'Those fullas in Wellington were hot on a nuclear power plant for the Hokianga, and we beat them on that one.'

For all the demands of her voluntary work, Fiona took care not to overlook Tom. But she worried: he was asthmatic and their place up the valley was cold and damp; it rained every day from April to October. Fiona knew she'd never have the money to put things right with the house. When Tom was four and his wheezing got worse they moved back to Auckland, the city Fiona had left seven years before.

Fiona still phones Sophie. But it's five years since they saw each other last, at a Green Party conference in Whangarei.

'There's a car ferry from Rawene, Tom.' Fiona is being patient. 'On the north side of the harbour we turn left for Mitimiti where my friend Sophie lives. You coming or not?'

Tom considers his options. 'I suppose.'

As usual, he doesn't have much to say but there's no sign of the iPod today. North of the harbour the land is different, drier – sandy and, in places where the conditions allow, there is plantation radiata. For Fiona life here would be a matter of sticking it out, like the stunted vegetation, against the sea and the prevailing wind.

For Fiona. But not for Sophie. She's waiting outside her fibro house as if she knew exactly when they'd arrive. She is seventy-five years old, a small woman but – Fiona is glad to see – still straight and undefeated, unless the deep crease that comes and goes between her eyebrows marks an unhealed hurt.

'Fiona. Haere mai, girl.' After a long embrace, Sophie turns to Tom. He's gathering his gear, taking his time. 'Kia ora Tom. I bet you won't remember, but it's been twelve years son.'

Tom could be about to shrug but his mother catches his eye and holds it as she moves, arm-in-arm with Sophie, into the porch. 'Shoes off, Tom.'

The house is small. A room for cooking and eating and living, a bedroom, a bathroom that looks like an afterthought. From the kitchen window Fiona can see a cobwebby outhouse. She'd feel penned in this place.

'Not much space, ay? At least we can't lose you here, Kui – that's my moko Miriama talking. Room to get lost out there though.' Out there, across the road, is the beach. Beyond that the Tasman. And Sophie does seem unconstrained, as if the walls of her little house were glass. Fiona sees a white stick propped in the angle of the wall by the door. Awareness builds for a few seconds before it hits her like a shockwave. Five years ago, Sophie was only talking about needing new glasses.

Miriama, when she comes from her mother's house along the road, kisses her grandmother and Fiona. Tom gets a kiss too, and a smile. Till now he's kept up a staunch disinterest in girls but, Fiona thinks, this one could break through. She's lovely: her elegant neck, her fluff of black hair, even her small feet as she kicks off her scuffs at the door.

Tom's blushing and a faint tic has started at the corner of his left eye. It's a reaction Fiona's seen before – as far back as Playcentre days when maybe he wanted to join in and didn't quite dare, or perhaps the supervisor had singled him out for special praise. The little twitch, and a sideways look at Mum for reassurance. He's doing that now.

'You fullas want some kai?' Miriama has already lit the gas and put water on to heat.

Sophie smiles. 'She's a good girl, this one – always around when I need her. Don't know what I'll do without her.'

Fiona senses Tom's sudden concern, as if the young woman might vanish any second.

Sophie has picked it up too. 'Miriama's going down to Tamaki Makaurau next month,' she says. She lifts her head and her eyes seem to find a focus. 'She's going to the university to study earth sciences.'

'Te reo too, Kui.'

'I know, dear. I'm glad. But I've got you for a few weeks yet.'

Miriama has been feeding them rewana bread and mussels. Tom's always detested shellfish but today he can't get enough.

'I want to show you something,' Sophie says when even Tom has stopped eating. 'We're going to the beach.'

Sophie takes Fiona's arm as the four of them cross the road. 'Tell me what you see.'

'A track through the dunes, the beach. The sea. Am I missing something?'

'This is the path to Te Rerenga Wairua. The last walk to Cape Reinga.'

'I thought the spirits gathered further north, on Ninety Mile Beach.'

'Our dead come from all over. But the west coast ones walk this way, they come past here.'

They're moving along the shoreline. Away south the sandhills bulk, bleached and combed by the wind. Northward, the beach stretches to a distant headland dancing on foam. The sun is high and hot. The lines of surf keep surging in.

'They leave us signs. Look,' Sophie says and releasing Fiona's arm she moves away up the beach to where the pingao grass knits the sand.

'Gran can't see much any more, but she *can* see the spirits.' Miriama lifts her hand and touches two fingers to her own eyes. 'They talk to her. Since my koro died. But she'll tell you about that.'

Her grandfather, Eru. Sophie's husband. Fiona knew him slightly. He used to pick Sophie up after meetings but – like Tom – never had much to say. Not in life, at least.

'Fiona, tell me what you see here.' Sophie is calling, pointing with her stick at wind-battered clumps of flax along the low ridge behind the beach.

'The flax? Strange, isn't it, how the wind has twisted the leaves together?'

'Not the wind, girl. The dead, telling us what we need to know. Can you see how the pingao shows you where to look?'

The grass does suggest a pattern, a pointer that pulls Fiona's eye to the knotted flax. But the spirit path? Poetry, not reality.

Sophie reads Fiona's silence. 'I know, girl. I'm a crazy old woman. But I reckon you won't argue with the message.'

'Mum!' Tom is calling. 'Miriama is going to show me where I can get coverage.' He holds up his cell phone and points down the beach.

Fiona waves, turns back to Sophie. 'What message?'

'Sit with me.' Sophie crouches and pats the sand.

Fiona squats; the sand is dry and warm, but not black with iron, not burning as it is on some other west coast beaches she knows. The wind flings grains at her, stinging her skin. She flops back on her elbows, digs in with her feet and squints between them at the long lines of surf. She hunts for a horizon past the spindrift.

'We're losing the beach,' Sophie says. 'Soon there'll be no path for the departing ones.'

'Erosion, you mean? Storm surges?'

'Both. Bit by bit, the sea is stealing the beach. There's more rain now.

More flooding. The sand is being washed down to feed the sea. Walk along the beach with me now girl, while we can.'

On the firmer sand, where the wind lashes her face and arms with spray, Fiona has to shout over the roar of surf. 'There's so much beach. It's hard to believe it could ever get... swallowed up.'

Sophie's grip on her arm is intense. 'In the last two years...' but she's talking about other, personal losses '...my eyes have gone. And my Eru. His tangi was at Whirinaki. Straight after, I came back...' the wind tears off a few words, then relents '...thought I'll just stay here a while, work on my sadness. I'm still working on it. Know what I mean, girl?'

'Yes.'

'The first day, my moko brings me to the beach. We walk, just like this, me holding onto her.' She gives Fiona's arm an extra squeeze. 'And I see them coming up the beach.' Sophie turns and gestures in the direction of the two young people, distant stick figures. 'I can't tell how many; they're shimmering... like a car coming at you along the road on a hot day.'

Fiona has to fix her gaze, to concentrate. Still, she can hardly distinguish Tom from Miriama, or even be sure they're two people.

'They come closer. Then I can't see them any more, they're faded into the haze.' Sophie rolls her damaged eyes, indicating the saturated air that erodes detail even for those whose vision is not impaired. 'I can still hear them though. It's Eru, his voice talking to me. All of them are calling to me, but it's only his voice I understand.' Those eyes are filling with tears. 'He's telling me the path is getting hard to find. Soon it will be lost. He wants to wait for me but he can't. He says he's afraid I won't be able to find the way when my turn comes.'

Back at the house, Fiona makes the tea. They continue to talk of climate change but Sophie is her old self again. 'This one's too big for those fullas in Wellington,' she says, and laughs.

When Tom and Miriama come in they bring with them a feeling of restless energy, and the bellowing of the surf.

'You hear that?' Sophie nods her head at the open door. 'At first I loved the sound of the sea. But when I got used to it, I stopped hearing it. Until…' she puts two fingers to her eyes, the same gesture Miriama made earlier '…these went. Now I hear it all the time. Can't get away from it, ay.'

Fiona puts two mugs of tea on the Formica table where the teenagers are sitting closer together than they need to. Tom has drawn a map and is writing his and Fiona's Auckland address above the diagram. The two heads almost touch as they lean over the scrap of paper.

'We'll have to go soon Tom,' says Fiona.

'A bit longer, Mum?' he asks humbly. Polite as he was at eight or nine.

Fiona glances at Miriama and her grandmother. 'Okay. I can see you've got these two on your team. As long as we make the last ferry back to Rawene.'

'Relax girl.' Sophie gets to her feet to close the door. 'You've got time.' The house is quieter then, with the wind shut out, though Fiona can still hear – like the muffled beat of Tom's iPod – the insistent pounding of the surf.

Summer Love

Graeme Lay

'In the hotel? In the *bar*?'

'Yes. I start tomorrow.'

'But it's such a *rough* place, dear, the hotel.'

'I'll be in the private bar. That's not so rough.'

'Perhaps not. What do you think, Edward?'

Stephen's father lowered his newspaper. 'I suppose it'll be all right. Clive Harrap's not such a bad chap, compared with some of the publicans we've had.'

There was a pause, then his mother said, 'But Stephen, you mustn't drink *yourself*, while you're working there.'

'Oh no.'

And that was how Stephen met Theresa.

For his new job he wore a long-sleeved white shirt, a black clip-on bow tie and his charcoal suit trousers. The Criterion Hotel was on the corner of the street above the beach. The private bar was a smallish room carpeted in a dark orange shade, with eight small square tables, each with four vinyl padded chairs and a large inset ash tray. There were windows on two walls of the bar, but high up so that people couldn't see in from the street. Every morning before opening time the bar was vacuum-cleaned by a slow-moving girl called Lois, but no matter how hard she vacuumed, the smell that hung about the room never disappeared. The pervasive smell was thick and sweet, a cloying cocktail of the bar's most popular drinks – beer, sherry and Pimms – mixed with cigarette ash. Stephen liked the indelible smell because it represented a combination of everything his parents disapproved of. They drank only sherry, and did so only once or twice a year.

But the thing that he liked most about the pub job was the surprising discovery that there is no more popular person in a bar than the barman. His customers greeted him like a lifelong friend. They chatted affably, asked how university in Auckland was going, shouted him drinks ('And have one yourself, Steve'), they thanked him profusely when he wiped down their tables. It was as if the booze he dispensed was his very own and he was giving it to them out of the goodness of his soul, rather than it just being a job.

As Christmas approached trade became brisker and the clientele of his bar more varied. Many of them were from other parts of the province, campers who had arrived early to get a good possie at the beach's camp ground. Clive Harrap's wife Dot put plaited gold and green paper streamers up around the bar, dangled red pompoms from the ceiling and a silver tinsel Christmas tree on a stand at one end of the bar. Stephen was kept busy filling up the beer glasses from the plastic hose and jigging shots of spirits from the row of inverted bottles above the bar. Between five and six o'clock Clive would join him to help cope with the clamouring customers. It was two days before Christmas when Stephen first served Theresa McGuiness.

'Two vodkas and orange. With ice.'

She was slender, with teased blond hair, pale blue eyes, a small neat nose and light freckles on her prominent cheekbones. She was wearing a pale yellow sunfrock and he could see the outline of her breasts through the cotton material. Eighteen, nineteen perhaps, he thought as the jigger squirted the vodka into the glasses. Not old enough to legally be in the bar, he knew, but who cared about that? Clive certainly didn't. Stephen was only just legal himself. The girl was avoiding his eyes, looking distractedly around the bar. Her mouth was well-shaped, her lower lip prominent. The pout gave her a sullen look which Stephen found very appealing. What would it take to make her smile?

'There you are. That's half a crown.'

'Thanks.'

As he took her money he noticed her bright pink nail polish and the fine gold hairs on her pale arms.

'Are you staying at the beach?'

'Yeah. Camping.'

'I'm Steve. How long are you staying?'

'Ten days. Till January the fifth.'

'I'll probably see you round then.'

'Yeah, see yuh.'

She half closed her eyes, her sulky expression replaced by a slightly sleepy, very knowing look. Then she carried the drinks back to the table where a red-headed girl of about the same age was sitting. They both drank in a self-conscious way, looking around the bar so that their eyes focused on no one in particular. But Stephen knew that she knew that he was interested in her. The next time she came up for a drink he would ask her to the Boxing Day dance at the Town Hall, which was a block away from the pub, five minutes' walk from the beach.

The tent that Theresa shared with her friend Darriel had been pitched under the big Norfolk pine tree near one end of the campground, which occupied the broad, grassy foreshore. Like almost every other canvas tent it was white and square, with a peaked green roof. There was no floor to the tent, just kikuyu grass. Dresses hung from hangers attached to the centre pole and on the ground on either side of the pole were double air beds covered in sleeping bags and blankets. Between the head of the airbeds was a wooden chest of drawers with a gas lantern on the top. Pots, pans and piles of plastic plates were stacked beside the tent door and a line of swimming togs, towels, panties and bras had been pegged out to dry on one of the tent's guy ropes.

He had arranged in the bar that afternoon to meet her at the dance. She had turned up at the hall at nine o'clock, wearing sandals, tight white shorts and a lemony-coloured top. She still wouldn't look him in the eye when he came up to her, she just gave him her distant, almost disdainful look, the one he found irresistible. And when he asked her to dance she just nodded, then looked away.

The band played mostly slow numbers and the lights were turned down low. She still didn't speak to him but as they danced he drew her close to him and he felt the bones of her hips moving against him. She put her face against his neck and nibbled it, and he caught the whiff of scent and cigarette smoke. He put his face in her hair and it smelt of scent too. 'Let's go down to the beach,' he said, into her ear. They disengaged, then, taking his hand, she led the way.

They were still dressed, although he had kicked off his shoes. Theresa began to writhe under him, seeming to move in several directions at once, like a frantic animal, but not one that was trying to escape, and now the fragrance coming from her was not bottled scent. She tore off her top and shorts, then helped him haul his trousers down. He hurled them away, then remembered that the packet of condoms was in the back pocket of the trousers. He got up to get them but she continued to clutch him. *'Steve! Steve!'* she was urging as he reached out and groped for his trousers. As he rubbed her, his mind raced. He had to get a condom on before it was too late. There was no way that he was going to do it without one. *Jesus Steve, come on, come on!*' She was grabbing him, holding him, dragging him down.

He was half way there when he knew it was too late, he began to teem, uncontrollably. Seconds later, spent and gasping, he rolled off the air bed. Theresa sat up and began to wipe her stomach with her knickers. 'Jesus, Steve, what a mess.'

He made a clicking noise. 'Sorry … sorry I messed it up.'

She stopped wiping and grinned at him. He felt sweaty and messy and whacked. They both smelt feral and disorderly. But it was also delicious. He liked Theresa's wantonness and frankness and her animal scent. That she was the sort of girl he could never take home, was another reason for liking her. Still wiping, she said, 'I suppose it's better that it went here instead of in the other place.' After Stephen threw himself back, helpless with laughter, Theresa looked puzzled, her small face and body gleaming pale in the moonlight. 'What's funny?' she said, letting her knickers drop into her lap.

'You are,' he said. He leaned over and put his face into her hair. 'Let's go for a swim.'

For a whole week she was part of his life. She came to the bar in the late afternoon, and after closing they walked down to the beach. They watched the Mardi Gras concerts with a blanket wrapped round themselves, they went to the Town Hall and danced only with each other. Darkness masking them, they swam in the sea at high tide before midnight, sinking into the silky water, then ran shivering back to the tent and threw themselves onto the air bed. His aim improved. Darriel had found a bloke of her own and had moved into his tent, so they had hers to themselves. Then he would walk home, exhausted but elated, at between three and four in the morning, and sleep until eleven. He learned something of her other life. She was a hairdresser in Ashtown. She was a Catholic, had gone to a convent primary school and had been a boarder at Sacred Heart College in Wellington. She still went to Mass and confession, she told him, and to prove the point on the Sunday after they first made it together she went off to Mass at Kaimara's Catholic church. When he asked her that night if she had confessed to the priest about them doing it, she looked puzzled at the question.

'Yeah, 'course. You have to.'

Stephen was seized with panic. The local priest, Father Muller, knew his father.

'Do you have to say who you did it *with*?'

'Oh no. You just have to say, you know, forgive me Father for I have sinned, I've slept with a boy.'

'No more than that?'

'No.' She gave him a playful punch on the shoulder. 'I didn't say, "His name is Stephen Lowe and once he came all over my stomach", if that's what you're getting at.'

'Then what happens?'

'Then he tells you how many Hail Marys you have to say, then you're forgiven.'

'And all ready for the next round.'

'Yeah.'

Laughing, she slid her hand down inside his shorts.

Although his family was Protestant, Stephen had to confess to himself that it wasn't at all a bad system. And Theresa being a Catholic made things wickeder and more thrilling, as if he was trespassing in more than one way as he savoured her forbidden fruits. Because of his bar work they met only at night, so that she seemed to him to be an entirely nocturnal animal. The Criterion's private bar was open to the public until six o'clock and for the hotel guests until nine. Then Clive would release Stephen and he would go home to have a shower and change.

'What are you doing tonight dear?'

'Going down to the beach. To the Mardi Gras.'

'You're spending a lot of time at the Mardi Gras this year. Is there something special on?'

'No, just the usual.'

'I see. Well, don't be late, will you?'

'No, no. Bye. Bye Dad.'

'Bye son.'

And off he would go to the beach, armed with his packet of French letters.

She clung to him in the dark like a baby possum as they sat watching the town's female impersonator, chubby milk bar proprietor Ron Janzen, prancing around the Mardi Gras stage in his feather boa to the strains of Begin the Beguine. Stephen and Theresa had a blanket wrapped firmly around them. He liked having his arm around her, liked feeling her slim body snuggling up against his, liked anticipating what they would do later in the tent under the Norfolk pine. On the fourth night he surprised himself by blurting out, as she writhed beneath him, 'I love you.' Then, jolted by the significance of what he'd said, he wondered why he'd said it. Putting her arms around him, Theresa said breathlessly, 'I love you too, Steve.'

He tried to let it pass, but couldn't. Sex was fine but love was quite different. You knew how it often ended. Marriage, quite often. Hell, not that, he thought. Especially if you *had to get married*. That would be a disaster. Anyway, Theresa knew he was at varsity, knew that marriage was out of the question. Hadn't she once murmured, as they made love, *I don't want to tie you down, Steve. But I do love you.* And he had checked, then, to ensure that the condom was firmly in place.

But now that she had declared her love he became worried about how it would end. She must have had lots of lovers, many more than he had, he could tell by the way that she showed him different things to do, but she never mentioned a current lover and he didn't ask. He didn't like to think about anyone else enjoying her lively little body the way he was. Hated to think of it. He wanted her to himself. Entirely.

He smiled at her from behind the bar and she wriggled her fingers at him. In two days she had to leave the beach and go back to work in Ashtown. He was going to miss her, there was no doubt about that. They had had so much fun. And she was going to miss him, he supposed, because she had told him several times how much she loved him.

They lay in the tent on the airbed, listening to the sound of the nearby waves and the revelry from the Mardi Gras area. Somewhere much closer, from a caravan over by the campground cookhouse, an Elvis record was being played. 'Wooden Heart'. He liked that song. Everything felt soft and warm and natural and musical. The summer night, the beach and sea, the lilting song, the soft, pliant body beside him. It was turning out to be a great summer.

'Theresa,' he whispered, his mouth against her ear, 'I love you.'

'Yeah Steve, I love you too. I don't want this to stop. Ever.'

The long, satisfying silence that followed was broken by the sound of a car, coming towards the tent, its engine in low gear. It came very close, then stopped. There was a pause, then a door slammed. They heard the sound of footsteps and breathing, outside the tent. Both of them stiffened.

'Theresa?'

A male voice, throaty and demanding. Theresa sat up, looking around wildly. Grabbing her pink nightie from under her pillow, she clutched it against her breasts. Then she froze, watchful and alert. Earlier in the evening they had laced up the tent entrance from the inside. The voice came again.

'Theresa? Are yuh there? It's Brian.'

She drew breath quickly, between clenched teeth. Stephen put his face close to hers.

'Who is it?' he whispered.

'Brian. Boyfriend,' she whispered back, her voice sounding panicky. 'Hang on Brian,' she called in a wobbly way, 'won't be a minute.' Looking at Stephen with wide eyes, she whispered frantically, *'You'll have to go.'* She looked around wildly. 'Go out under the tent. Over there.' She reached over and picked up his clothes. *'Take these with you …'*

The voice from outside the tent came again, louder, with an edge of menace now.

'Jesus Theresa, what are yuh doing? Get the fuckin' tent flap open, will yuh?'

'Coming Bri, won't be a sec…' She pointed at the rear wall of the tent. *'Off you go. Quickly!'*

Stephen's heart heaved. He stared at her in astonishment. She had told him that she loved him, now she was telling him to scram. *'Why are you doing this?'* he hissed. *'What about me?'*

She threw up her hands.

'I didn't know he was coming here. But I have to let him in. He's been balloted into the army. National Service. He's going to Waiouru this weekend, for three months, *and I want to have his car while he's away.'* She sat up, clipped her bra back on, went to the rear wall of the tent and lifted it up a few inches.

'Go on, get out!'

The next day, before starting work, he walked to the cliff-top. He looked down at the beach, the campground and the place underneath the Norfolk pine tree. There was just a square of flattened grass. Where her tent had been.

Pararaha

Charlotte Grimshaw

Beth and Per lay near each other on the sand. All along the beach the heat haze wavered and danced. The only sound was the roar of the surf.

Marie was digging a hole. Her sunhat kept falling over her eyes. It was a nuisance. She tugged it off and screwed it into a ball. They were always making her wear the nasty, floppy thing, even though it made her itchy and covered her eyes. And it was hideous. Marie liked to look nice.

She looked carefully at her parents. Per had his chin on his hands and was staring down at the sand, concentrating. Beth lay face down, her head on her arm. Their calves were lightly touching. Slowly, Per reached across and rested his hand on the small of Beth's back.

Marie swiftly rolled the hat into a sausage and poked it down into the hole. She took her spade and filled it in, patting the sand over it. Then she flopped quickly down onto her stomach and lay very still, holding her breath.

Slowly she turned her head. No one had noticed.

A girl sprinted up the beach and leapt onto her towel, reaching down, exclaiming, to hold her sore feet. Marie listened to her shrill complaining – the black sand got so hot that you had to wear shoes. Once they'd met a tourist who'd set off in bare feet and got caught in the heat on a long stretch of beach. He was in a terrible state, his feet badly blistered and burned.

Three figures were coming across the dunes. Marie watched the mirage splitting the figures apart into silvery bubbles. At first they seemed to be floating above the liquidy blur made by the light, but as they got closer they solidified and shrank and turned into a man and a woman and a girl wearing straw hats and carrying coloured beach towels. The woman leading, the man and the girl stumping along behind.

The Brights, Robin and John, trailed by their daughter Caroline, greeted Beth and Per. They dumped their gear and sat down in the sand.

Beth rolled over and said lazily, 'Isn't it divine.'

Robin took Caroline by the arm and smeared suntan lotion over her in swift efficient dabs. Caroline smiled at Marie.

Marie hated and feared Caroline. She was a big girl – her sister Emily's friend – who never lost a chance to deliver a vicious poke or kick when Emily and her parents weren't looking. Once she had forced a big piece of mud into Marie's mouth and then said in a shocked voice, 'Look, Emily, she's eating dirt,' and had rubbed Marie's face extra hard, pretending to clean it. Marie spat into the sand at the memory, and crept closer to Beth. She was terribly aware of the buried hat, inches from Caroline's foot.

John Bright solemnly coated his nose with white zinc. He stretched out his skinny legs, dug his long white toes into the sand and began to sing in a deep bass voice:

Home, home on the range
Where the deer and the antelope play

'There,' Robin said, pushing Caroline away. To Marie she said, 'Would Marie like Caroline to take her to the lovely lagoon?'

Marie shook her head. No thank you very much.

Caroline, who had been gazing dreamily into space, looked suddenly interested. She eyed Marie's soft little arms, so satisfying to twist and pinch. What fun to poke sticks into a small foot, to see the mouth open in howls of infant distress. Caroline got a hot delicious feeling just thinking about it.

She said casually, 'I'll take her if she's not too shy.'

'Would Marie like to go and make lovely sand castles?' Robin asked Marie.

The little blonde head shook emphatically. No, Marie would not.

'Would Marie like a nice little paddle?'

Marie pushed her face into Beth's shoulder. 'No.'

Robin said, 'I vowed that Caroline would never be shy. I exposed her, socially, from a young age.'

But Beth said, 'You go ahead, Caroline. I'll bring her along later.'

John's singing rose above the murmur and roar of the sea.

Where seldom is heard

A discouraging word

And the skies are not cloudy all day.

And Caroline, thwarted, gave Marie a terrible, meaning look and slouched off across the hot sand.

'Where are your other lot?' Robin asked, arranging herself comfortably on her towel.

Beth said, 'They've gone on a bush walk. We're meeting them down here.'

Per looked up. 'Actually, you'd think they'd be here by now.'

They all scanned the beach.

'They should be coming around the south rocks,' Beth said.

'Where have they been?' Robin asked.

'It's a track. The Pararaha Gorge. They're meant to come around the shore.'

Robin said, 'The Pararaha Gorge? That's a tall order. Who's taking them down there?'

'They're by themselves,' Per said.

'By themselves?' Robin almost shrieked.

Beth rolled over. Per stared.

John elbowed himself up. He said carefully, 'The Pararaha's an eight hour tramp. It's a very long way. It's rough terrain too.'

There was a silence.

Robin's eyes were bright. 'Didn't you know?' she murmured.

Beth hugged Marie. She looked fearfully at Per. 'It was a project of Larry's. He thought it up. He's so sensible; he's got a map. And they wanted something to do with Sam.'

'Sam?'

'We're minding him. The Richardson's Sam.'

'But he's only five,' Robin said. 'Do you mean to say that three children aged ten, seven and five are…'

Per rounded on her. He said in an iron voice, 'It seems we've made a mistake. You're saying they're too young.'

'It's an absolute marathon. And there are cliffs and rapids and and…John?'

John nodded. 'It's a tough one,' said the deep voice gently.

Beth picked up Marie. She said, 'Oh God. Per. What should we do?'

Per said, 'I'll go round there.'

'Round where?' Beth said.

'Round the rocks. To see if I can meet them. And if I can't find them you'll have to call the ranger.'

Beth rocked Marie back and forth.

Robin shaded her eyes. 'Here we go,' she said, waving out.

A smiling couple lugging a chilly bin between them came staggering across the sand.

'Over here,' Robin called.

And to Beth and Per she said brightly, 'Well. Here come the Richardsons.'

They were crushed. There was no more track, just a sheer drop. Larry had got such a fright that his face had a greenish tinge. Sam immediately caught their fear and began to wail drearily. There was nothing for it but to turn around. They walked all the way down the bluff, until they were back at the river bank.

Emily had begun to hate the river. It laughed at them, dashing along over its rocks, it menaced and mocked, it teased and flaunted itself. She threw a rock into it, and slipped and grazed her foot, and the river babbled and sighed and chuckled to itself.

She and Larry searched for another track. They were wary of entering the really dense bush; they knew how easy it would be to become confused, especially here where the gorge had widened out and there were gullies and dips in the terrain.

They gave up and sat down, bathing their feet in the stream. The sky was still bright but the colours were changing, the sunlight growing yellower as the afternoon wore on. It wouldn't be many hours before shadows started to cross the rocks. Emily thought with fear of the bush at night.

Larry frowned over his map. Sam bleakly ate the last sandwich and Emily stared down into the tiger-striped shallows, where the water rippled over ochre stones and the weed waved, and the eels curled and slipped between the rocks. She saw a crayfish poke its claws out from under a rock as if to check the underwater weather – the swirls and flurries of sparkling mud, the tiny leaves whirling lazily past its door. And shot back under the rock again, quick as a flash. The feathery river weed was combed and parted by the current, and tiny bubbles of air were caught in its strands and lifted off, and whisked away.

Larry said, 'I've got it.'

She looked up.

'It's obvious. We're so stupid.'

He got up, snapping his fingers. 'We don't *have* to find a track. All we have to do is follow the river. We want to find the sea, that's where the river will take us.'

Emily got up, pulling Sam. Larry paced around them, repeating himself. 'We've wasted all this time trying to find the track. All we need to do is follow the river. It doesn't matter if the track's disappeared. '

He was so convinced that Emily and Sam felt a flicker of hope. Sam heaved a long watery sigh. Emily dug her fingernails into her palm and prayed to the Unknown Somebody that Larry was right.

They went on. When the riverbank gave out, they waded and swam. Larry tried to carry the pack on his head but it was soon drenched, and they simply dragged it or floated it ahead of themselves. The water was cool and fresh; they sank in brown mud, slipped and slid over stones. They swam in their clothes and shoes. Where the river was flowing too fast they clambered along the bank, hanging onto the ferns.

Now that they had given up searching for a track they felt they were making progress. Sometimes they could lie in the water and let the river carry them along, sometimes they swam and waded through long slow lagoons, where the nikau palms grew thickly overhead and the water lay brown and sun-striped and sluggish. Emily watched her shoes kick up the mud in little golden bursts.

There were fewer rapids and waterfalls now. The land had begun to flatten out and they were no longer walled in on both sides of the river by steep hills. The afternoon sun blazed down, the bush was still in the heat, light glinted off every leaf and the cicadas were so loud that the air seemed to shimmer and vibrate with the sound. There was still no sign of a track but they kept faith with Larry's idea: a river must lead to the sea. As long as they stuck with it, they wouldn't get lost.

Emily saw a plane high in the sky, a tiny silver dart. And she saw that shadows were starting to cross the bush. Now they were walking through a kind of grassland; the river was broad and slow and there were little tributaries, marshy pools, banks of toi toi sticking out of the middle of muddy bogs. Larry shouted from up ahead, and when she and Sam joined him they saw that the track had resumed, winding and overgrown and pitted here and there with the hoof prints of cows.

'Listen,' Larry said. They could hear a distant sighing roar – the sea.

They were in a wide, shallow valley. There were tussocky paddocks, fields of low scrub, and in the distance black and white cows, grouped under a tree. Water lay everywhere, in brackish pools along the edge of the path, fringed by great banks of native reeds. They passed pools filled with bright green weed, and tiny green frogs sitting motionless on lily pads in the shade of the waving stalks. The heat was intense. The sun was lower and burned into their faces. They were so tired that they couldn't talk.

They came to a sign. Larry consulted his map and Emily couldn't raise the energy to kick him or to ask him how far they had to go; she only looked at the sign with dull resentment; she thought there was something utterly shameless about the track, the way it had simply resumed, all cheerful and business-like, without a word of apology, as if it hadn't abandoned them in the middle of the bush.

And now, finally, the sea was really roaring, and when they crossed a wooden bridge over a marsh and followed a narrow path under a row of cabbage trees, they came to the foot of a vast black sand dune. Emily looked up the glittering iron slope to the intense blue sky. She had never seen such a dune, a monster, its spine curving like the back of a giant lizard, its rippling flank so black that it had a sheen of blue.

They began to climb, toiling up the slope, their feet sinking into the hot sand. Sam began to cry as the sand got into his sandals, burning his feet. They reached the top and there before them was the huge curve of the coast, stretching many miles south, all the way to Whatipu, and to the north towards Karekare, a desert of black sand and dunes and scrub rippling with heat waves, and, far across it, fringed with surf, the wild sea. Emily turned and turned; it seemed to her that the whole landscape was full of bright, violent motion. The fluffy toi toi waved in the wind like spears borne by a marching army, the surf ceaselessly tumbled and roared, the light played on the sand, casting a powerful, shimmering glare. Where the black desert met the land there were enormous, grey cliffs that sent the sound booming off them. Behind them lay the green valley they had come through, with its marshland and cabbage trees and the river that had spread into many waterways, spilling out towards the sea.

They walked along the backbone of the great dune, and across a boiling expanse of beach. They plodded, sinking into sand, scrambling wearily up and down dunes. Then they came down into a trench of scrub under the cliffs, where cabbage trees grew along the edge of a stream, and pohutukawas hung off the cliffs. Here they were screened from the roar of the sea by the dunes, and there was a path of hard, matted grass that was easy to walk on.

But Sam sat down with a bump. He couldn't go on.

Larry climbed up onto a clump of dune and scrub.

'I can see people,' he shouted.

She joined him. Far away, near the sea, there were figures walking in a line. Little shapes against the dancing, glittering water. Fishermen or trampers, heading for Whatipu. She saw that the light was changing; there were clouds gathering on the horizon, streaked with greenish light. Soon the clouds would turn orange and the sun would go down; there would be no twilight, no lights, only the sudden, absolute dark.

'Look what I got,' Larry said. His hand was full of bright, squashy blackberries. There were clumps of bushes, laden with fruit. They picked more and carried them back to Sam. The little boy dragged himself up with a persecuted look and consented to trudge on, his mouth stained with red juice.

Emily saw something ahead, a circle of light against the headland. It was a tunnel, cut out of the rock, made a long time ago, Larry said, reading from a blurb on his map, when there was a railway line around the coast.

They walked through the tunnel, running their hands over the cold stone. 'Now we're nearly there,' Larry said when they came out the other side.

But Sam sat down again, and this time he wouldn't move.

'Christ,' Hugh Richardson kept saying. 'Christ.'

He was lucky, Per grimly reflected, that Hugh was too civilised, too repressed, to give him the tongue-lashing he deserved. All he could do was explode every now and then with a little wounded exclamation. '*Christ.*'

The two fathers had crossed around the rocks and now faced the immense wasteland of sand, stretching away in the polished light towards Whatipu.

There had been a scene on the beach. The Richardsons' mounting alarm, Beth's anxiety and remorse. Per had felt utterly sorry for Beth and blackly furious with himself. He couldn't even remember the discussions that morning about what the children were doing; he had assumed that

Beth was handling all that, and of course she had been distracted, and hadn't understood what Larry and Emily were meaning to do, and now they were somewhere in this huge landscape or worse, lost in the bush or drowned.

'Bloody hell.' Hugh loped along next to him, shading his eyes. 'It's going to get dark.'

Per looked along the line of coast and felt a part of himself crumbling with misery and panic. Should they go back and call the ranger, the police – summon more help? Now they'd come this far it would take a long time to get back, and meanwhile the dark would come on. He couldn't go back – it would be wrong to turn away and leave them, even if it was the rational thing to do.

Images floated in his mind. The jolly smiles fading from the Richardsons' faces. Marilyn Richardson bursting into tears. The children in sunlight, waving as they walked away.

They joined the track. Four fishermen appeared near the cliffs and Hugh scrambled towards them, holding up his hand.

'Have you seen three kids?' he called. 'Three lost kids.'

The fishermen conferred rapidly in their language, shook their heads and marched past. Per stared after them uneasily, wondering why they were so taciturn. Was there something shifty about them? The fronds of the cabbage trees rustled over their heads, as sharp as knives.

Per looked up at the wall of rock, at the deep black spaces. He felt as if the cliffs were ringing with a terrible sound. The iron echo rang in his head. The whole landscape was reverberating, crying out to him. The crash of the waves on the shore, the cliff-echo. The black rock, the black sand, the seagull shifting on its red feet, its shiny black eye with no light no depth in it.

There was an orange tinge to the sky now. Long shadows crossed the sand and a cool wind came off the sea.

They passed through a manuka glade and came out on a long stretch of scrub and marram grass. There ahead of them they saw three small figures, sprawled in the grass at the edge of the track. They rushed forward.

But the children's faces were covered with blood.

Hugh's shout, the surge of his own blood, the horror and fear. Per ran and ran. He reached them first and they held up their little smeared hands. Blackberry juice.

'Christ,' Hugh exploded for the hundredth time, swinging his boy up into his arms.

Per would never forget it. It would stay with him. He would make sure of this, by writing it down. The ringing of the cliff, the wild sound, the iron song the land had sung.

He took his children by their red hands and thanked the God he didn't believe in, thanked Him anyway.

(from) Hummingbird

James George

Jordan lifts his tattooed chin to the air, opens his lips to taste then slides once more beneath the waves. He dives, kicking with his feet, cutting through the sea's skin and into its veins. He twists, rolls over and over, lets the oxygen drain from his lungs. Then he rises above the surface again, drawing in the scent of salt on the wind, opening his pores to the air.

A half hour later he sits on the beach, a surfboard wedged in the soft sand beside him, its form casting a spearpoint of shadow. He glances up the beach to the dunes. Nowhere is there any evidence of other people. Neither a fence, nor a marker post. Even the few tyre tracks have been blown over by the sand-seeded wind. A lone pohutukawa has a foothold on a small ridge, its overhang painting the gold of the beach a darker hue, as if a shadow tree, attached like a Siamese twin, grows in the sand. He sits away from it, avoiding even the suggestion of leaves on his skin, wanting only the invisibility of water.

He stands and jogs down to the tide, carrying his surfboard, entering the waves without slowing. He takes aim toward the north, where the high and low tide lines parallel each other to the horizon.

An hour's walking then a run into the ocean to surf, then another few kilometres on sand, an alternating road of land and sea. At the sight of the hill with its broken face he quickens his pace, peeling off through the shallows to arrowhead out to the deeper water, riding the current back in, looking for that one homebound wave. When he finds it he grabs its tail: breaker, board and rider a single figure. He aims for the line of dunes, a halo of surf breaking around him. He is almost to the shallows when he glances up beyond the jetty to where the shape of a vintage aeroplane sits in the sun.

Kataraina climbs the ladder onto the boat, goes into the cabin and lifts the guitar from the bed. She carries it outside, sits cross-legged on the deck and begins to play. Again she fumbles at first, but then begins to reach out along the breakwaters of her memory, her fingers seeking sanctuary among the frets. Her movements are slow, allowing each touch against string, each fretted tone to ring. She pauses, raises her hand to wipe away a few strands of hair which the sea breeze has blown over her eyes, then goes back to her music, unaware of anything peripheral to it until a shadow crosses the skin of her arms. A hint of footfalls on creaking wood. She glances up, expecting to see Kingi, but instead it is a young man, wearing only a ragged pair of shorts. She looks up the length of his muscled frame to his face where tattooed wings of ink rise from the bridge of his nose, half circling his eyes. The arcs of ink echo around his lips, his stubbled chin; their deep forest tinge matches the pounamu pendant on a string around his neck. His eyes search not her face or body but the fall of her fingers on the strings. She tries to meet his gaze, but he will not meet hers. She slows her playing, an arpeggio filling the empty space between them.

He glances to where a surfboard stands staked in the sand. She looks at it, suddenly conscious of the touch of sea water on her toes, dripping from his body. He crouches in front of her, still looking at her hands, his rust-coloured eyes seeming empty of any greeting, but bearing no anger either. They hold nothing but her reflection. He makes no move to claim the guitar from her, or even speak. He stands again and climbs back down the ladder to the sand.

Kingi fingers the oily surface of the bearing, wincing when a torn shard cuts into his fingerprint, oil mingling with the sudden bulb of blood. He flexes his hand, reaches with his other hand into his breast pocket for his handkerchief. He spits into the cloth then dabs at his finger, looking up when a young man's figure appears on the dunes, the line of his body fractured by Kingi's view through the wing struts. The man pauses in front of the open engine compartment, glances down at the propeller resting on the right lower wing. He lifts it and runs his palm along the edge of one blade, its surface angled like an oar. He walks the length of the fuselage to the tail then crouches behind it, looking up its length.

'Another traveller,' says Kingi, 'or would you be the landlord?'

'Neither. Just looking after the place till summer.'

'What's the going rate?'

'Rate?'

'For accommodation.'

'Beats me. No one's been by until now.'

'I might need to kip here awhile, to work on the Moth.'

The man nods, still looking at the aeroplane.'

'Whatever,' he says, then walks away up through the marram grass.

Kataraina wades in the shallows to the south of the stream, carrying the diary in her clasped fingers. She glances towards the horizon, where a cluster of dark clouds pass, far out to sea. She opens the diary and raises it to the sun, taking a single page between her fingers, looking through the weft of the paper. She brings it to her nose and sniffs. Dust, perhaps a dim trace of grass. She closes the diary, turns to look back to the north where the surfer lugs an old dinghy out onto the sand.

He drags it through a tangle of driftwood, tails of seaweed forming a wake. He steps inside it, sits on the cross member, reaches into the hull and lifts up a small wooden block about the size of a fist. He takes a torn strip of sandpaper from his jeans pocket and wraps it around the block. Kataraina picks her way through the shells towards him. He glances at her sandaled feet. The etchings in his skin radiate in the sun, as if a stone has been dropped into the pool of his face.

'I remember when old Porangi Sam had that boat you're staying in,' says Kataraina.

He runs the sandpaper along the hull's lip.

'My grandad,' he says.

'Te Awa? Shit, you're one of them?'

He looks up at her for the first time. 'Yeah,' he says. 'What of it?'

She blinks. 'Nothing,' she says. 'Just wondered sometimes, where you all got to.'

He goes back to his sanding. 'Scattered all over the place,' he says. 'You know how it is.'

'Yeah. I do.'

She steps sideways among the seaweed, folds her arms. 'That's a beautiful guitar you've got,' she says. 'Did you carve the lettering on it?'

'Nah. Bloke I once knew.'

'Once?'

'You're a big one for questions, huh.'

She turns to the trees, then back to him. 'You want us to leave?' she says.

'Us?'

'Me. Him.'

'It's up to you.'

Jordan spends a couple of hours sanding the dinghy. Parts of it are worn so smooth with countless waves that they are the texture of bone. He lifts his hands every now and then and shakes his fingers free of dust, then carries on. He glances up along the beach to where the old man tinkers with his biplane, oblivious to the passage of a four-wheel drive that slows to look at him, fishing rods and a dog hanging out of the rear tray. Jordan watches the ute pass, the driver flicking a hand in casual wave. He makes no gesture in return.

Mid-afternoon he stands back, aware now that the wood dust hazes about him when he shakes it free, an onshore wind building. He drops the block and sandpaper on the floor of the hull, steps out and walks to the riverbed and collects his surfboard. Within minutes he is in the waves, entering them with the gentle timing and ease of a lover slipping within the skin of another. He rides one crest then goes in search of another, a balance in the line of his body, from his toes to the tips of his fingers.

Kataraina stands in the dunes, watching the surfer's shadow captured within the fabric of the water. His outline as fleeting as a wavetip. She bends and scoops a handful of sand, then opens a slight gap in her palm to let it slip free as she walks from dune to dune, the sea-wind blowing the falling sand against her. She raises her hand high, letting the last of it go, looking through a curtain of sand at the surfer losing himself in the waves.

She had sat in a bar in Kings Cross in Sydney, her elbows on the beer-stained table, staring at the strobe lights reflected in her margarita. She'd never qualified as a true alcoholic, though she'd tried pretty hard, really just for dramatic effect. Poets and painters who became drunks were known as bohemian. She liked that, it had a nice ring to it. But even that she managed to screw up. Only Kataraina could try to have a lost weekend but end up remembering every tedious minute of it. Right about then it struck her that Kings Cross, which had never brought her happiness, was also a lousy place to be miserable.

When she sighted the first hint of coastline from the 767's window she'd leaned forward, watching the folds of sea turn to lacings of whitecaps. She had wondered if the first explorers had stood in their canoes and marvelled at that same sight. She turned to the other passengers, some reading newspapers, some packing their papers back into their bags. Mothers wiping the faces of infants. She was glad no one bothered to look up and see the wetness at the edge of her eyes.

She'd picked a spot and drawn an X on the window with her lipstick and watched its tilted cross drift over the land. When the ocean and pasture gave way to cityscape she leaned back and closed her eyes. She wasn't interested in the shadows of buildings.

The Paua Gatherers

Maurice Shadbolt

After dinner, after the third and worst argument of the day, he vanished behind a slamming door.

The crisp pretty black-haired girl found small things to do. She passed dishes through soapy water and whisked a broom over the floor. When the condition of the flat satisfied her, she felt calmer, more in control. She went to a couch, relaxed on cushions and raised her eyes slowly to the closed door.

She could wait now, smoking, reading and listening to the clock on the mantelpiece. Or she could walk. After all, it was Sunday, the day lonely people idled through city streets. Eyes would watch from shabby doorways as her heels ticked through the streets; ticked her past lifeless window displays and aimless people. But when she returned the door would still be closed against her, and the silence heavy.

A small hysteria rose: she felt trapped in this room, this flat, this city. She jerked to her feet and snapped on the radio. A solo saxophone jazzed into the grey afternoon.

There was a sound of protest from his room. Her fingers strangled the saxophone. She lit another cigarette, looked in the mirror, removed a fleck of tobacco from her lip, took up a book, riffled pages and placed it down again. She stubbed out her cigarette in the iridescent bowl of a paua shell ashtray and walked to the window.

The city lay below, the houses strewn around the harbour and heaped up the hills; the scene was cheerless in the flat winter light. Her first view from here had been different, on a warm summer day with a cool breeze along the narrow wooden streets. They stood at the window together, seeing the dappled buildings under blue heat-haze, the dark harbour shimmering beneath straw-coloured hills, white yacht-blades cutting calm water. In a rare mood of enthusiasm for the discovered flat, the new city, Tim took her arm.

The girl stood at the window alone. She imagined how he would be now: tense while the point of his brush discovered line, fidgeted with colour. And she, in this room, waited confused, uncertain, unable to settle, only knowing that summer had gone, that it was winter, and she was alone. 'There are books,' he would say with a vaguely irritated gesture, indicating the titles cramped along the shelves. 'You can read, can't you? Other people find something to do with themselves, don't they?'

Other people found something to do with themselves.

There was a knock on the door. She woke to the present, to the wind in the curtains.

Ted stood on the steps; she was glad it was Ted. He was Tim's only real friend, a rolling stone who moved about the country from season to season, beachcombing with Maoris in Northland, sheelite mining in the Alps, cutting tourist tracks at Milford Sound. Lately he had been living in the city; he was their only visitor.

He grinned from his black-bearded face and, duffle-coated, a small canvas bag swinging from a shoulder, he slouched in the door. 'And how are the kids today?' he said cheerfully, in his soft Irish voice.

She tried to smile in the particular way she always smiled at Ted. But quite suddenly she was blinking back tears.

He slipped his arm about her and helped her into a chair. 'There,' he said. 'What's all the trouble now?'

'Nothing, really,' she said. 'Nothing, Ted. You just got me at the wrong moment. That's all.'

'There now,' Ted said. He dabbed lightly at her eyes with a red handkerchief. His face gentle, he stooped over her, one arm still about her comfortingly. 'Better?'

'Yes, Ted. Better.'

'The old man locked away again?' he said. He sat down, crossed his legs and began to fill his pipe. Ted never worried for long; she liked him for it. He was a comfortable person; he always put her at ease. She liked Ted to keep her company.

'Yes,' she said. 'He's busy.'

'What's the masterpiece now?'

She shrugged, wondering if Tim had been listening behind his closed door, and felt a dead weight of tiredness.

Ted looked at her curiously, and changed the subject. 'Well,' he said, slapping his knee. 'What do you say to a meal of paua tonight?'

'Wonderful.'

He looked at his watch. 'Low tide's at four. I better get weaving. It's an hour out to the beach from here.'

She hesitated. 'Would I be a nuisance if I came?' she said quietly. 'I'd love to get out –'

'Fine,' he said. 'I hoped you'd come.'

'Then why didn't you ask me in the first place?'

'Because I like people to please themselves.'

She heard the slap of Tim's sandalled feet; his door sprang open. He emerged smiling, cool and tall in his paint-smeared black sweater; the front patchy with tobacco ash.

'How's the boy?' he asked Ted.

'Just fine.'

'Going somewhere?'

'After paua. And Ann has just decided she'd like to come along with me.' Ted seemed oddly apologetic.

Leaning in his door, Tim lit a cigarette. 'Good idea,' he said casually. 'But it's a hell of an afternoon to go after them, isn't it?'

Ted shrugged. 'Maybe they'll taste better today.'

Tim laughed shortly; she sensed tension between them. She hurried into the bedroom and returned zipping a windbreaker.

'You have to go right away?' Tim said.

'Why?' Ted said. 'You want to come too?'

Tim shook his head. 'I'd like to,' he said.

'Then why not?'

'Too much to keep me busy.'

'Give it a rest. It's time you got out of that room.'

Tim looked doubtful. 'I'll see how I go,' he said. 'I might just follow you out to the beach.'

'Right,' Ted said.

The tram jolted towards the beach. Ted, remembering the tears, wondered whether today was after all the best time to speak to Ann. Perhaps not; it would be taking unfair advantage. And anyway he was not sure yet that he would be able to say what he wanted. She might not understand; she might turn away.

Yet today he had her alone, clear of the flat, even if only for a short while. It might be his chance.

The tears had surprised him. They could mean that everything was ending after all; that all he had to do was wait. But first he would have to be sure of the words, sure of the time.

There was no sign now of the tears. Her face, nipped by the wind, glowed; twists of dark hair tangled from under her yellow head-scarf. She darted glimpses of the passing suburbs through the dusty tram window; and, talking to him, her quick hands gestured.

Curious, she and Tim. Yet what kind of a girl should he have expected for Tim? And which Tim?

The first he remembered clearly. They met in Auckland – Auckland, that impassive city sprawled casually over a green South Pacific isthmus – not long after he arrived in the country; in the dust and dag-stink of a woolstore. New to the city, a refugee from an austere and lonely childhood on a depressed backblocks farm, that first one had been shy and timid. It was an achievement, after the small beginnings of friendship, to persuade Tim to show the work which obsessed him.

He helped Tim, encouraged him, found him a better place to live and work, loaned him money for paint and brushes, sketchbooks and canvas; and introduced him to others who might help. And when he was satisfied he could do no more, that Tim had all he needed, he went deer-culling for a year.

And then he found the second one. More assured, Tim moved with confidence in a fresh circle of friends. They met more as equals now.

On Saturdays, under dark walls hung with yellowed pictures of forgotten racehorses and boxers, they drank together in a small waterfront pub where they joked with their friends – Josef, the Dalmatian fisherman; Harry, the retired burglar; Andrew, the disillusioned evangelist turned alcoholic. For Tim they were friends only now; no longer subjects. His subjects were after the fashion of his other friends.

Then there was the third. The seemingly taller Tim, almost a stranger, who had shaken off all friends, not only the simpering hangers-on, the corduroy theoreticians, but even too the friends of the waterfront pub (because there was his work, his paintings built with blocks of violent colour knifed with heavy lines). Yet they found their way back to friendship.

Finally, after a long spell out of cities, Ted discovered him gone from Auckland; there was the story of the girl who had left with him.

'A skinny little bitch,' Hans, an effete Continental poseur, had told him. 'Absolutely characterless and uncreative. Out to suck him dry. You see.'

'She might do him good,' Bridget said hopefully, examining her long cigarette holder with interest, when Ted went to her flat.

'You think so?' he said, while wondering if Bridget was remembering her own affair with Tim; she had been Tim's first woman.

'She's only a child, really. But you never know, do you?' Bridget's plucked, pencilled eyebrows arched with question. 'She might be just what he needs. There's something gone wrong with him somewhere, hasn't there, Ted? Inside him, I mean. When I remember that time you first brought him up to see me – ' She made a small gesture of despair. 'I don't know. Do you?'

The tram banged to a stop. 'Here we are,' Ted said. They swung down from the footboard.

The suburb was sunk in peninsula hills at the end of the harbour. They climbed clear of the houses and a road led them down through a cutting to the open sea. Then the beach, bleak and deserted, spread in a grey sweep below them. The ebbing tide left reefs of black rock.

They took a thin path down to the beach. The coarse sand rasped underfoot as they picked their way across.

With the wind flushing her face, she turned to Ted, laughing. 'Know something?'

'What?'

'Who cares if we don't find paua?'

'Me. I like them.'

'And I just like getting out, getting away – ' She stopped, suddenly aware that she had said too much. 'I like that smell of the sea,' she added lamely.

'Who doesn't?' he asked, grinning easily.

She was surprised at her own calm.

He helped her over the rocks, his hand brown around her pale wrist. Then, seeking the grey-shelled paua, they peered into shallow green rock-pools and into crevices where the sea still swirled.

2

They had been gone an hour. He still couldn't call stop. He should get out, look around, let everything fall into place again.

It would be too easy to lose his grip. There were enough irritants already.

Yet he was sorry now for what had happened. He couldn't blame her for anything. She followed her logic; he followed his. It seemed impossible to express himself clearly anywhere but here, and then only by way of bitter geometry.

For too long he had lost himself among other people. That was why he had come to this new city, to find himself again. But people still confused him; left him unable to see things calm and clear as he had once.

He needed to be alone, free of her. For her good and his. That was what the geometry said.

Without thinking, he had slipped into a coat.

Then why lie to himself? If he really wanted to be free, why follow them? He knew Ted too well not to know what was happening, not to know why Ted had stayed in the city so long. On Saturday afternoons, when they drank together, their desultory conversation and bleak pauses only reminded him of conversations when they laughed at themselves, at each other, and felt no hurt.

Then Ted could have her, he told himself.

So why follow them? The dead faces and wooden seats in the jerking tram gave no answer.

At the terminus he met the bite of sea air. He began to walk briskly through the suburb. Then he slowed, seeing suddenly the neat homes in the Sunday quiet, the gaunt trees against the sky, two boys riding a trolley, a squall of small girls with tumbling curls and dangling dolls, an old woman forking a grey flower plot to chocolate. How long since he took notice?

He climbed above the houses and into the cutting, frowning, bewildered at himself. Walls of yellow clay parted to reveal the beach, the surf along the long margin of sand. He saw two distant figures moving about on a stubble of rock.

He paused, thoughtful; then he stepped down from the road, where they might have seen him. Screening himself behind patchy scrub, he slid down the bank by degrees, nearer to the beach. A little way above it, he sat on a rock, his feet resting comfortable on a curve of clay.

Their voices were faint: from where he sat he saw them framed by fern and broom.

Gulls circled noisily above them as they searched.

'His trouble,' Ted was saying, 'is that what he's doing is hypothesizing himself out of life. He's got the fool idea into his head that he has to get clear of it to look at it properly. Ideas about ideas. No rough edges, no mystery. It's all cold and hard.'

'Yes,' she said, and then was silent.

'I'm boring you.'

'No, Ted. Not at all.' She raised her eyes above the sea to the wheeling gulls. 'Ted,' she said quietly. 'Do you think he loves me?'

The sea sucked at the rocks.

Ted, head down, avoided her eyes. Like a woman, he thought. Always it had to come down to the personal.

'Do you think he can?' she said.

Ted shrugged, watching the confused weed tangle up in the swell. 'Don't ask me,' he said.

'Be honest. Forget you're his best friend.'

'He's too reductive to be seductive.'

'But it doesn't have to be like that – not always, does it?' Because, she thought, Tim was not like that, not always.

'We're not doing much good here,' Ted said. 'Best to move on a bit. The tide'll beat us if we don't find something soon.'

Light was seeping from the afternoon; and the pleasant feeling had left her.

'I wish I could do something to help,' Ted said, reaching out to lift her over a broken shoulder of rock.

'Thanks Ted, but there's nothing.' Of course there was nothing; why persist? But it was one thing to be logical; another thing to leave Tim.

Ted rolled his trousers and waded into new crevices. She stayed above him, pointing to where she thought she saw the colour of the shells among the surging weed. Then he would feel underwater, knife in hand, for the paua. He found some small ones. 'They'll do,' he said. 'If we don't find more.'

Presently he straightened, hands on hips, the sea washing about his knees. 'The tide's coming in pretty fast,' he observed in a flat voice.

'Is something worrying you?' she said.

'Me?' He laughed, without conviction.

'Something is worrying you, isn't it?'

He didn't answer; she watched him climb slowly from the sea.

3

He was building it carefully now. Their two figures in the foreground; and behind them the sky, the thin light on the sea, a spray dancing over black rock, a flight of gulls and a far-off fishing launch. The emphasis strong, their colours rich against the leaden day.

Ted, stooped, would be gathering the shells into his canvas bag, his bag curved, the blue tartan shirt falling loosely about his waist, his brown corduroys lifting above his pale bare ankles, the black of his hair flowing to the stub of his beard; the pipe jutting, the face absorbed and serious.

And Ann? Standing, looking down at Ted, arched slightly, the headscarf fallen loose and yellow about her neck, the open green windbreaker snapped by the wind, revealing the red sweater beneath, the gentle line of the small breasts. The air cascading about the face. The face half-hidden.

Why not? He had no paper, no sketchbook; he began to draw on the back of a cardboard tobacco packet, working through the idea before it left him. He looked up to see that they had moved further along the beach. Their voices were lost altogether now. In a moment he would join them.

He thought he might speak to Ann then. Instead, scrambling from the sea, he dried himself and pushed the shellfish into his bag. She said nothing; she merely watched him curiously. Too conscious of her, his thick fingers fumbled clumsily with the bag. He closed it, slung it on his shoulder, and suggested they walk a little way along the beach to see if more paua could be rescued from the rising tide. He did not look at her.

'Tim didn't turn up, after all,' he said. Why should he feel guilty? He had said nothing, betrayed no friendship.

'Has that been worrying you?'

'Why should it worry me?' He discovered an irritation in his voice.

'It has been worrying you, though. Hasn't it?'

'It would've done him good to get out,' he said irrelevantly. 'He never gets out. Cooped up in that room all the time.'

She was silent. The sea hissed under the darkening sky. She felt spray on her face.

Suddenly he swung about to look at her; his face was agitated. 'All right,' he said. 'So you know. You needn't be so damn smug about it.'

She looked bewildered, hurt. 'What?'

And then he saw, and was sorry; she had not seen.

'What is it? What have I done?' Her words lifted away in the wind. But she knew.

She felt chilled and tired. Ted's voice was quiet; she could scarcely hear it above the sound of the sea.

'I'm sorry,' he said. 'I just wanted to have a talk with you this afternoon. It doesn't matter about what. It doesn't matter now.'

'What doesn't?' she asked.

He looked at her.

'Getting dark,' he said. 'Shall we get moving?'

He jumped lightly across a gap in the rocks, then waited to catch her. 'All right?' he said, observing her curiously.

'All right,' she said.

She jumped. Her feet slipped on greasy rock; a sob leapt unexpected from her throat and tears stung her eyes. But Ted's arms caught her before she fell. He swung her up to him, and planted her down firmly. She clung to him; he did not push her away.

'It's all right,' she said, recovering.

He did not release her. His hand slid gently down her loose hair and then, with sudden urgency, lifted her face. He was warm against her, and gentle; his lips tasted faintly of tobacco.

Then he let her go.

'I'm sorry,' he said brokenly. 'I forgot myself. It's just that –' He raised his arms in appeal, then let them fall, helplessly. 'I'm sorry.' He turned away and she caught at his arm, despairingly.

He saw them come together, the two figures in the fading light, to become motionless, silhouetted singly on black rock above the white lines of surf. Presently they moved along the beach, becoming indistinct against the darkened sand. Then they were lost to sight behind a finger of land. He scrambled down to the beach, trying to catch sight of them again. Sand slid under his feet; he stumbled and pitched forward. He rose and ran along the beach, the sea in his ears. But he saw only a grove of pine and a derelict boat-shed. He stopped running. Breathing heavily, he looked towards the shed. Then he looked down to see that one hand had fastened tight around sand. He opened the hand and let the grains dribble between his fingers. Then he turned stiffly and walked away.

4

The wind, creaking through the pines, slapped the broken boards of the shed. He could hear the waves beating over rocks, up the sand.

Her white face was lost, her body withdrawn into the darkness.

'I expect we'd better go now,' he said. His voice sounded faint to himself.

'I'm sorry,' she said presently.

'For what?'

'You've got to understand,' she said.

'What?'

'That –' She hesitated.

'That it doesn't mean anything?' he said. 'Because I know that already.'

He slumped back to the floor, turned his face to a chill draught of air. Escape was one thing; sanctuary another. He was familiar with the first. He might learn to live with the latter.

'I'm sorry,' she said. 'It's my fault.'

'We can go now,' he said presently, but he made no move.

'Yes,' she agreed. She was calm. She reached for Ted's hand and found it. 'Yes,' she said. 'We can go now.'

From his room he listened to them enter the flat. The tap of Ann's heels, the scuff of Ted's heavy shoes. He heard them talking in the kitchen as they prepared the meal, hammering soft the paua steaks.

He concentrated again. Glancing at the crude notes on the tobacco packet, he worked quickly, building with thick strokes of black pencil. Then he was lost. The figures were angular, the rocks inflexible too.

From the kitchen he heard the hiss of gas, the pop of flame. Presently the smell of frying steaks seeped into the room. He heard percolating coffee, the low voices.

He began again. It was better; the stiffness was going. Important that he understood.

She called his name.

He held the drawing to the light. It was rough still. The incoherence mattered less by the minute.

She called his name again.

He seemed to have mislaid anger.

Ted had built a crackling fire of resinous pine. They sat before it, eating the paua.

He congratulated them on the meal, tried to joke with them. Ted smiled weakly. Ann was aloof. So he fell silent too.

Ann rustled through the silence as she cleared the dishes and poured coffee. When she finished she sat cross-legged on the floor between them. She was wearing slacks now, and a black sweater, and looked trim and neat and boyish.

'Working on something new?' Ted said finally.

'You might say that.'

There was no large interest apparent in Ted's face.

Tim began to feel desperate. Running a hand abstractedly through his hair, he tried to summon up conversation.

Then he saw they were both looking at him.

At least not at him. At the sand which showered from his hair.

He affected not to notice.

5

Ted stood at the door. His pipe fixed between his teeth, he gave his full attention to fastening his duffle-coat. 'I meant to tell you earlier,' he said. 'I think I'll be pushing off this week.'

'Pushing off?' Tim said. 'What's the hurry?'

'No hurry. I've just been thinking lately it's time to push off north again. It'll be warmer.'

There was a pause. Tim looked at Ted.

'You don't really have to go, you know,' he said.

Ted lowered his eyes and fidgeted with the top fastening of the coat. 'I've been here long enough. Time to be moving on again.'

'I wish you didn't have to. I'll certainly – I mean, we'll both certainly miss you.' Tim was aware of Ann standing beside them. 'You'll see us again before you go, won't you?'

'I'll try,' Ted said. 'But I'll probably be busy. I might just push off tomorrow, or the day after.' Ted thrust out his hand suddenly. 'So here's just in case.'

The handshake was austere. Ted's eyes looked dead. Tim wished there was some way to reassure him. There was no way.

'We'll be seeing you down here again, won't we?'

'Sure thing,' Ted said, without conviction.

He opened the door. Thunder slammed beyond the hills and lightning made the horizon vivid. New rain began to spit through the darkness.

'Anyway I'll be able to get in touch with you?' Tim thought at last to say.

'Through Bridget, probably.'

'Bridget?'

'She seems rather on her own now.' Ted shrugged. 'Besides, she promised me a job on her magazine. Any time I wanted it.'

'And you want it now?'

'I didn't say I wanted it.'

'But you used to say that was one kind of thing you'd never –'

'I used to say I'd never do a lot of things.'

Through the open door they looked out upon the wind and rain, the growing storm.

'I'd better go,' Ted said.

Ann spoke at last. ''Goodbye Ted,' she said quietly.

'Goodbye.' Ted raised a hand in salute. 'Be seeing you.'

They watched his back disappear into the rain and dark, heard the dwindling sound of his footsteps. The front gate clicked shut.

Tim closed the door. Ann switched off the radio and turned to face him. They were alone now. The fire crackled and rain hissed on the windows.

'I'll sleep on the couch tonight,' she said simply.

He turned away, without hope.

'Whatever you like.'

'And I'm sorry,' she said.

'For what?' he said, swinging sharply.

'For everything. For you.'

'I don't want sympathy,' he snapped. And more quietly added, 'I expect you'll be going too.'

'Surprised?'

'Not really. With Ted?'

'No. I'm not going after Ted. You heard what he said.'

'Then where?' he said, perplexed.

'Home.'

'Home? Back to your people?'

'Back to my people.'

There was a silence. He looked at her bleakly.

'I'll marry you. If that's what you want.' He might have meant it.

'But don't you see?' she cried.

'Not enough, apparently,' he confessed.

Outside, the first of the storm was spent.

'You have the bed,' he told her finally. 'I'll take the couch. I'll be working late.'

'Shouldn't you get some sleep?'

He shook his head. 'I've got something to finish.'

'At this time of night?'

'To start, then.'

He turned into his door.

'Tim,' she called.

'What?'

'Nothing,' she said.

'Nothing?'

'Coffee?'

'That's be fine. Thanks.'

'Much to do?'

'Too much.'

He swung his door shut and she raised her eyes slowly, with dull dread, to see it close against her for the second time that day. Remembering Ted, she gave a small cry, too low to be heard, and darted to the window. But there was only the rain; the rain on glass, and bright lights bleeding.

The Rip

Christine Johnston

They never intended to go swimming that afternoon, and had ended up on the beach quite by chance. The scariest thing, Lou would think later, was the way one unplanned event *seemed* to lead to another, and to produce some kind of momentum, when in fact, as everyone knows, a chain of random events is neutral – good luck and bad luck are equally possible, and nothing is predetermined.

The day had started badly – with heavy summer rain drumming on the roof, making the beach a most unlikely prospect. As there was no food in the flat and a mess in the kitchen, Lou suggested to Jack that they go out for brunch.

Then they quarrelled. Lou discovered that while she was in Whitcoulls, Jack had bought five CDs.

'You're always complaining about being short of money,' she said sharply, turning away and refusing to look at the titles or comment on his choices.

Two were second-hand, he commented, though he hated being called to account for his impulse spending. They weren't married, he reminded her, as he did quite often, which Lou found infuriating. (He'd asked her once when he was drunk and she'd turned him down.)

She didn't say much as they walked back to the car, except to comment that the rain had stopped. Jack put one of his new CDs in the player and instead of going back to the flat, drove in the opposite direction.

'Where are you going?' asked Lou, shouting over the music.

'Anywhere,' he replied.

They quarrelled again and he told her she was turning into a nag. She should lighten up. She thought about getting out of the car and walking home. Sometimes it was all too much – riding in Jack's car, listening to Jack's music, being Jack's girlfriend.

When they spotted Pete and Mel walking along the one-way with bags of shopping, Jack pulled over to pick them up and put the bags in the boot. At Mel's place he invited Pete to come for a spin and although Mel seemed reluctant the four of them set off with the stereo blasting, out to the motorway and along the picturesque south coast where big waves broke only a few metres from the road. They stopped the car more or less at random and walked the short path to the sea.

The beach was deserted. Lou launched into a series of cartwheels. She loved that headlong, almost out-of-control feeling. In the open she felt all the tensions evaporating. Jack was fun to be with outdoors. They only ever argued in confined spaces – in the car, in shopping malls, in restaurants.

They were walking among the debris left by the summer storms, when the sun broke through the clouds and it was suddenly hot. They stripped off to their underwear. Jack and Pete began searching through the flotsam, seeking out logs and tree trunks and planting them upright in the sand. Pete set about attaching horizontals, making arms by lashing branches with lengths of kelp. Jack found a blue plastic float with a few metres of rope attached. Pete was excited about the idea of constructing sculptures from the abundant driftwood. There should be four figures, he suggested, versions of themselves.

Lou and Mel joined in, collecting seaweed, branches and shells to decorate the figures. Lou had taken off her dress, a cotton shift, and she hung it up, threading a switch of willow through the armholes. It flapped in the breeze, but gave the tree trunk an eerie life of its own. Mel, clad in T-shirt and panties, and Lou in her underwear and a black slip, worked together on this figure, which soon sported a head made from Mel's balled up shorts, seaweed hair and an ice cream pottle hat. The four of them worked happily for half an hour in the bright sunshine, but Jack was too much the engineer to be satisfied with a sculpture and began to dismantle his construction.

Lou and Mel were still busy on the female figure when they became aware that their boyfriends were now talking about 'buoyancy'.

'What are you doing?' asked Lou.

'Change of plans,' replied Jack. 'We're working on something a little more technical here – a craft of sorts.'

'A crafty raft,' added Pete.

'You're not planning to put it in the water?' Mel's voice had an edge to it.

'I don't think there's any danger the thing will float,' laughed Pete. 'Don't fret. Our chances of ending up in South America are slim.'

'They'll be all right,' said Lou. 'Jack's a strong swimmer. Let's finish our goddess and she can watch over them.'

'You look a bit like goddesses yourselves,' said Jack, grinning. 'Sure you don't want to climb aboard? We need some ballast.'

'Well, thanks a lot, Jack.' Mel flushed with anger. She had a womanly figure with wide hips and a generous bosom. She turned away, but Pete came after her, wrapping his arms around her until she pushed him away.

Behind their backs Jack and Lou exchanged glances.

'Come on, sailor,' Jack called. 'Let's see if she's seaworthy.'

Jack and Pete dragged their raft into the surf. They tried to mount it but it tipped over, dumping them in the water. Jack's laughter rang out. Lou went to where Mel was sitting on a log. She was surprised to see tears in her friend's eyes.

'Jack didn't mean anything personal,' she said, fetching her cigarettes and lighter from her denim jacket.

'Do you mind not smoking?' asked Mel. 'The smell of it makes me chuck.'

Lou looked at her in surprise. 'Are you …sick?' she asked.

'No.'

'You're not …?'

'Pregnant? Yes, I am. Well and truly.'

'Mel.'

Mel pulled up her T-shirt so Lou could see the bulge below her navel. Her breasts had got larger too.

Lou sat down beside her, tossing her Rothmans into the sand. 'God, Mel.'

'Yeah.'

Lou fiddled with the lighter. 'Jack didn't mean anything.'

'Yeah, I know.'

They looked at Jack and Pete wading into the surf, pushing the raft into the breaking waves. It lurched sideways and returned to the shore.

'Pete's such a kid,' Mel sighed.

'What'll you do?' asked Lou.

'We're getting married at Easter.'

'Wow.'

Mel was so deadpan about it all. Lou, at a loss, searched her friend's face for clues.

'I think that's great,' she said finally and hugged her. Mel's skin was hot from sunburn, but her soft, womanly flesh felt strangely inert and passive. For a second Lou was distracted, wondering what it was like to be Mel's lover. What was it like to be Pete, making love to Mel? These were things you never knew. She didn't know what it was like to be Jack, either. It occurred to Lou that no matter how close you got to people, you couldn't get inside their skin.

'That's *really* cool. You're such a great couple. It'll be my first wedding since my dad got married, and that was year ten.'

'Oh, we're getting married in Auckland,' said Mel. 'It'll just be family.'

Lou was stunned. 'Well, good luck anyway.'

The two friends were silent. Mel put her hand on Lou's bony knee.

'If I was having a bridesmaid, *you'd* be it. But …'

'No worries.' Lou was thinking, they've made all these plans and never said anything until now. 'So, when does baby arrive?'

'August.'

'Wow.'

'Yeah, wow.'

Lou was counting back. It was already March and she reckoned it must have happened before Christmas. Mel had known for weeks.

'Are your parents all right about it?'

Mel was looking down at her bare feet. 'Yeah. They're cool about it.'

Lou laughed suddenly. 'Look at those mad bastards!'

Jack and Pete had dragged and pushed their raft beyond the breakers and were scrambling aboard. Jack waved triumphantly from a kneeling position, while Pete kept trying to get his leg up.

'And Pete's parents? How are they dealing with it?'

Mel didn't answer. 'Look at Pete,' she said.

He was on board but seemed to be lying down, holding on.

'Don't worry about them. Jack used to do life-saving. He's a good swimmer.'

Mel turned to Lou and gripped her arm. 'Pete *isn't*. And he panics.'

'Does he?'

'When I told him I was pregnant, he panicked. I mean, totally freaked out. He couldn't even talk to me for about a week.'

'What? Mel, that's terrible. How did you cope?'

'I coped,' said Mel, getting to her feet. 'All because his father's a big shot in the Christian Heritage Party.' She sighed. 'Totally pathetic.'

'I can't believe they got that thing to float,' said Lou. She followed Mel, who was walking to the water line. Lou caught up with her and took her arm.

'You love Pete, don't you?' she asked before she could stop herself. 'You *do* love him?'

Mel didn't answer. She just stood there with her bare feet in the shallows, and her hand raised to shield her eyes from the glare. There was something timeless and statuesque about her, Lou thought. She was *the woman on the shore*. Beyond the breakers the raft with the two figures bobbed uncertainly. It was being drawn out to sea.

Jack and Pete waved; Lou and Mel waved. Mel made an anxious keening noise, as they saw the raft moving away from them. Jack waved again, more wildly this time, and they could hear his excited laughter. He was having fun.

'Get off it,' said Lou, as if she was speaking directly to Jack. 'Jump off and swim back.'

Lou and Mel could see that the raft, cobbled together from driftwood, rope and kelp, was breaking up. As it went under, Pete shouted something to Jack, but they couldn't hear what he said.

Lou strained to find two heads in the water, but managed only one.

The waves were obscuring her view and she had to jump from time to time to see what was happening. 'They'll be all right,' she said, as reassuringly as she could.

'Pete will panic,' said Mel.

Lou's heart began thumping wildly. What if Pete panics and drowns? What if he takes Jack with him? 'I can see two heads now,' she cried. 'Jack's a strong swimmer.' She put her arms around Mel, who was rigid, standing with her legs firmly planted in the tide. What was it like to be Mel at this particular moment, trying to stay balanced, standing in the surging water, with a baby inside her?

'They're in a rip,' she said.

'They'll be all right,' Lou repeated.

Under her tan Mel had lost all her colour. She pulled away from Lou, took a couple of steps and threw up into the water. Although she had little to vomit, she retched repeatedly.

Lou looked away, looked out to sea. She saw only one head – Jack's – and he was stroking boldly towards the shore. Then he turned around. Lou could see two heads again. She waded out into deeper water, walking sideways towards the north, the way the rip was carrying them.

She saw two heads, one head, for a few seconds no heads at all. Then Jack's head popped up again.

'Swim!' she yelled. 'Swim to me, Jack!'

She felt vaguely ashamed and looked back at her friend who was still bent over, though she had stopped vomiting. Lou felt light-headed. Not able to watch any more, she left the water, stumbling on the damp sand. Finding herself on her knees, she started praying. 'Please God, save him,' she cried. She didn't care about Pete, she realised. She cared only about Jack. She bent lower, praying like a Muslim with her hands on the ground. She clawed the ground, the good, solid ground, terra firma. 'Please don't let him drown.'

She thought about drowning, about lungs filling up with water. She thought about death.

She saw Jack emerging from the sea. He was holding Pete, propelling him towards the shore. They both stumbled and collapsed. Pete was naked and shivering. Lou went to Jack and laid her hand on his wet head. Jack was too breathless to speak, and when he looked at Lou, she saw terror in his eyes.

'You're all right, aren't you?' she said. 'I knew you'd be all right.'

Pete was coughing, bringing up sea water. His movements were slow, as if he was drunk. He seemed unable to speak. Lou looked around for Mel. He friend was walking away from them and towards the tree trunk that was their goddess.

'We should get him into the car,' said Lou. It was late afternoon and the temperature was dropping. Jack stood up unsteadily.

'What a rip that was,' he said to Lou.

He grabbed Pete's hand and yanked him to his feet. With Pete's arm across his shoulder he dragged him up the beach to the dry sand. Mel was coming towards them, carrying the clothes they had abandoned less than an hour before. In a businesslike way and without a word, she dressed Pete in his shorts and sweatshirt, feeding his limbs into the clothing as if he was a child.

The three of them managed to march Pete to the car. Lou and Mel sat on either side of him in the back seat and wrapped a blanket around him, so that he looked like an elderly invalid. In the heat of the car Lou and Mel were sweating, but Pete's teeth still chattered.

Jack told them what had happened. He'd been able to swim against the strong undertow, but Pete hadn't. Every time they set off, Pete was pulled back. Eventually, in a last desperate attempt, they'd managed to launch themselves, and after that the waves brought them to shore.

Pete's eyes were more alert and he seemed to be recovering. Mel didn't ask questions or say very much, except to point out the sign they'd all missed, which said that the beach was dangerous.

'Can we go?' she asked Jack.

As soon as he started the car, the stereo blasted them with sound. Jack punched the button and silence returned. He drove back to town slowly, stopping at a bottle store to buy some beer. Mel asked Jack to drop them off at her place. Pete hadn't spoken but before he left the car he gripped Jack's shoulder.

'Thanks mate,' he said.

Lou got out of the car. 'Will you be all right?' she asked Mel.

She nodded. When Lou gave her a hug she felt a small convulsion like a sob inside her friend's chest. Mel pulled away and followed Pete inside.

When Lou returned to the car she saw Jack gripping the wheel and staring straight ahead.

'It was touch and go,' he said to Lou. 'I was running out of steam. I said, 'You've got to do it or you'll drown'.' I told him, 'You go first and I'll be right behind.' I had to push him off the sand bar. If he'd gone under again, I would have left him to it.'

Neither spoke for a minute or two. Lou took his hand. 'You made it, though.'

'Mel's a cold fish,' said Jack.

'She's pregnant,' said Lou. 'They're getting married next month.'

'Well, she was bloody near widowed this afternoon,' he said. He started the car.

When they got home, Jack drank some beer and lay down on the bed. Lou drew the curtains and lay beside him. She licked his salty shoulder.

'Were we lucky?' asked Jack. 'Were we lucky, or what?'

Free as a Bird

David Hill

Except for a few sawing and nail-banging noises three or four fences away, the rest of the baches were empty. The boy Darrin liked the emptiness. At least today his mother wouldn't be at him to go and make friends with the other boys. On this glittering winter morning, the other boys were back in their home towns, at school.

He went down the bank of springy kikuyu at the end of the bach's lawn in four jumps. Another two took him across the frontier of thinning grass where bank curved into beach. Three more, and he was over the creaking belt of driftwood and seaweed, bleached plastic bottles and orange twine that lay along the high-tide mark. He stopped to tug at one long stick where it poked out from a tangle of old fishing net, pushed it away when it refused to come, and went on across the grinding pebbles towards the rock pools.

Something was happening between his mother and his father. That was why they had all come to spend these four days at the McIntyres' bach; why he'd got nearly a week off school.

He'd heard his Auntie Diane talking to his mother about it. 'At least see if a different environment makes *you* feel different... Try and get Lance to look at it from a different perspective.' He didn't understand all the words; he knew he wasn't meant to, but they knocked unpleasingly in his mind.

He'd gone down to the rock pools yesterday, on his first day at the bach. He didn't think much of them at first – the scoops and sink-sized hollows with their pitted rims seemed ordinary and unpromising. But they made him bend to look into them, then crouch to see past the surface glitter of sunlight. There were stones and glossy seaweed underwater that needed his hand to move them aside. Winkings of tiny claws beside the stones. A flicker of transparent tail as a cockabully betrayed itself above the matching bottom of sand. Only when he stood up and felt the cramp in his knees and the fronts of his thighs did he realise how much time had passed.

So he came down eagerly to the pools this morning. More eagerly because he could feel the drag and crackle starting to build up, back inside the kitchen of the bach.

It was cold in the bach, too. He'd heard Mr McIntyre talking to his father. 'Now there's no excuse for not being warm. You've got extra blankets in the wardrobe, and that little fan heater throws out a real glow.' But his parents hadn't used the heater. They knew the McIntyres wouldn't accept any payment for the electricity, and they didn't believe in being in people's debt. He knew that before they went, his mother would make his father take the hand-mower out of the shed and do the lawns. She would sweep out both rooms, and wash the floors and windows. Even though nobody would be using the bach for another four months – he'd heard Mr McIntyre say so – they would leave it tidier than they'd found it.

Down at the pools, the boy Darrin stood and blinked in the blue-and-yellow day. The winter sun was on his back. The sea breathed beyond the rocks. Gulls lifted up as he approached, and circled with their long cries above him. He began making his picture come back, the picture he'd started on while he was down at the rock pools yesterday. In the picture, he was standing before his mother in some unspecified place, and speaking to her. The words he was speaking weren't specified either, but his mother had her head lowered. Sentences were stepping from him which somehow raised his father to the status of wronged victim. Sometimes in the picture, his father came and stood beside him while he spoke, and put a hand on his shoulder. But he didn't feel comfortable with that part. Now he was looking at a seagull. The bits of his other picture went thin and slid away. One seagull, floating silent and tidy in a pool quite close to him. It hadn't flown up with the others. It just sat in the water; its head was still while its body trembled a little on the surface of the pool. He began to move closer. Slowly, one step at a time. How near could he get before it took off? Near enough so it could see he was friendly? Near enough to touch it, even?

It was one of the small gulls. Grey feathers on its wings, a few black-tipped ones on its tail. He took another pace closer. The red beak ended in a little hook at the tip, where the top half fitted over. He'd never noticed that before. Another step. The eye was like little rubber rings, red on the outside, then white, red again, and black into the centre. Another step and another. The sun behind him. The seagull was hurt. Along its breast and side, just above the water, exposed pinky-grey flesh glistened in the sunlight. It's torn its guts open on a rock or something, the boy told himself. He edged forward with one hand outstretched, making little noises of reassurance.

Then he was lurching backwards, away from the pool. The wound of pink-grey flesh had crawled and twisted along the seagull's side. The bird's body dipped in the water, then rose again. The beak opened, but made no sound. The eye stared. He saw the line of white suckers along the edge of the tentacle, where it gripped the bird.

One of his heels was dripping blood where he'd jarred it against the rock rim. He made himself go forward again, staring. Once more, as his shadow touched the water, the tentacle tightened and gleamed. Down under the big rock in the middle of the pool, the octopus braced itself against a new presence. The gull dipped with the movement. It might have been floating on a carefree swell. The dazzle of sun made it impossible to see down into the pool.

He knew straightaway that there was one thing he couldn't do. He couldn't put his hands on the tentacle, and try to pull it free. What if he touched the clinging suckers? If the pink-grey flesh shifted sideways and came sliding up over his fingers and wrists? His lips drew back at the thought. A picture caught at him, and he was off across the rims of the pools, to the high-tide line of driftwood where the stick poked from its tangle of fishing-net. This time he didn't tug at the stick. He wrenched and tore till it came splintering away into his hands. He panted back towards the pool.

The bird was motionless again on the water. He knelt on the rock and stretched the stick's broken end out slowly till it touched the flesh of the tentacle. The white suckers wrinkled.

Next moment, he was lunging into the water beneath the bird. Jabbing and threshing and hauling the stick from side to side in the pool. His own body and head were turned away, his eyes closed against what might come writhing up the stick at him.

The water frothed and slapped over the rock rim, and the gull lurched on sudden waves. Sand and mud rose from the bottom. The stick met a resistance like a wet sack. He snatched his hand away, and clutched it to him. Bird and stick floated side by side on the surface of the pool. A second tentacle had joined the first, glistening along the gull's white side.

He turned his back on the pool and ran for his father. Across the pebbles and up the bank of kikuyu grass to the bach. When he flung in through the back door, his mother and father were sitting silent at opposite ends of the kitchen table. In the darkness after the sun outside, he couldn't tell at first who was which.

His mother's voice began to say something about dirty feet, but he went straight over the top of her. It was like the picture he'd been making for himself earlier.

'Dad! Dad! There's a seagull down in the rock pools, and it's caught by an octopus! You've got to get it out. The octopus is gonna drown it! Please, Dad, you've got to come now!' Then he was off again, running before demands for explanation could snare and delay him.

When his father joined him at the pool, he was crouched again on the rim, trying to look down into the water. The man, who'd come striding jerkily down from the bach, said nothing to his son. Instead, he picked up the stick that was floating at the pool's edge and pointed uncertainly at the gull. And the boy Darrin had another picture.

This one was from a month ago. Their cat had started choking on a fishbone. His father, who was nearest, had grabbed the animal and tried to pat its back. The cat twisted and squalled. His mother had said, 'Give it here! God, you're useless!' With the animal tucked under her arm, she'd reached deftly with finger and thumb for the fishbone. His father had walked out of the room.

Now his father was jabbing with the stick in the water, just as the boy had done, only harder with his man's strength. The boy saw the same things happen: the water lash and slop, the bird toss from side to side, the tentacles contract around it. But this time it was pulled deeper into the water, till its sides and folded wings were half-submerged. 'Don't!' yelled the boy. 'Don't! It's drowning!'

He knew instantly that they were the wrong words. His father's face went red and helpless. He slung the stick away so that it clattered and somersaulted across the rocks. Then he stooped and wrenched with both hands at a stone the boy couldn't even have moved. He rose, straddled above the pool, and lifted the stone high over his head.

'No, Dad! Don't kill it! No!'

The man stared at his son. He opened his mouth and eyes as the seagull had done. Then he dropped the stone back onto the pool rim, and was striding, running back up towards the bach.

The boy stared after him, hands pressed against his ears where they'd jerked when his father scooped the stone high. He was heaving to breathe. His eyes felt tight and bulgy.

Then – 'Dad! Dad! I know!' He too was off towards the bach once more. Blundering up through the kikuyu, reaching the top of the bank just in time to glimpse his father vanish inside the door.

He didn't go for the bach. Instead he snatched open the door of the shed where the lawnmower was stored. His hands scrabbled along the shelf for what he'd seen there yesterday – the pruning saw with its curve of rusty teeth.

He held the saw in front of him as he slid and stumbled back down to the pools. Both his feet were bleeding now from the pitted rocks. The seagull still floated silent on the surface of the water. The black centre of its eye stared at him.

The boy Darrin stopped at the pool's edge. Then he drew back his lips again and stepped in.

The winter water gripped him up to his thighs. But it was only two steps into the middle of the pool. He did what he'd known he could never do, and seized the seagull with one hand. He reached beneath it with the pruning saw, and began hacking backwards and forwards with the hooked blade. He yelled as he sawed, and he felt the rusty teeth jag and tear. The tentacles gripping the bird contorted, then whipped away. The seagull was free in his hands.

He still whimpered and shrieked till he was out of the pool and headed towards the bach, the pruning saw dropped somewhere in the water, the gull held against his body with both hands. But he was silent except for the heave of his breathing by the time he reached the lawn at the top of the bank.

The seagull had lain unmoving against him, all the way up from the rock pool. He would get it bread and a dish of water from the kitchen. Maybe there would be a tin of sardines his mother would let him open. But first the bird could rest where it was safe. He knelt down, and placed it gently on the soft grass of the lawn.

For a second, it sat as it had on the surface of the rock pool, body and eyes still. Then its beak opened for the second time, and stayed open. It shivered once along its length. A white membrane slid down over the eye nearest to him.

When the boy Darrin finally stood up, his knees and thighs were stiff with cramp, the way they'd been yesterday after he'd knelt and stared into the life of the pools. He reached out with one foot, and gave the seagull a push. The bird sagged over onto its side. For the first time he could see its breast where the tentacles had gripped and crushed. The white feathers there looked just as unruffled as they did everywhere else.

He moved towards the bach in the glittering sunlight. His feet were covered with sand and blood. His jeans were soaked, and he'd ripped one of the cuffs on his jersey. He supposed he should wash his hands and feet under the outside tap, but he couldn't be bothered.

This time when he opened the back door, it seemed even darker inside than it had before. Once more his parents were sitting at opposite ends of the table, and he still couldn't make out at first who was which. They weren't looking at anything, and they weren't saying anything. As he looked at their faces staring past each other, he saw again the eyes of the seagull.

My Beautiful Balloon

Carl Nixon

It is obvious to you that the chairs should be facing the ocean. You are standing on the crest of the last dune before the beach, looking out at the sand and the waves and the grey/blue Pacific. It is cold and you can see your breath in the air. You watch as a woman in a dark dress-suit and coat methodically places the chairs on to the sand.

She looks up the beach and sees you. She is probably wondering if you are the first to arrive. But no, your faded jeans and hoody belong to someone out for an early morning walk. The invited guests will be dressed formally, especially the Japanese dignitaries. The Mayor is also going to be there.

The woman turns away from you. A pile of collapsed chairs lie behind a black SUV that she has driven down on to the sand. The name of an event management company is printed on the side doors. She opens each chair with a practised flick of her arm and places it carefully on the sand. You watch until she has eventually constructed a tight crescent of thirty-three chairs – you count them – three deep, facing back towards a rostrum. The guests will be looking toward the dunes, which form a natural amphitheatre.

It is just past nine in the morning and the sky is cloudless. There is no wind and the scattered lupins near you on the dunes do not stir. Small waves fold in to the beach below. Above the ocean, like a pale hole in the sky, is the moon. It is only a day or two off being full although whether it is waxing or waning you do not know.

You look back at the woman and the chairs. The guests will be arriving soon. Surely, she must see that the chairs are all wrong.

* * *

There was an unusual mix of tourists and locals. More tourists was the norm but on that day it was half and half.

The two Japanese, Mr and Mrs Nishiura, were both short but he was even shorter than she was. His face belonged on a young boy, round and padded, although you guessed that he was in his early thirties. You remember her as being Asian-air-hostess beautiful.

The Nishiuras had been married the day before. They had been limousined around the city. It was their second wedding. The first had been in Japan with family, friends and work colleagues. Their exotic Kiwi wedding was really all about collecting photographs to show the people back home. The photograph that had been taken in front of the cathedral was printed on the front page of the following day's newspaper. You remember carefully cutting the photograph out. You still have it in the top drawer of your desk. Mrs Nishiura looks like a frail unsmiling fairy in her hired wedding dress. Mr Nishiura stands next to her in black coattails and a silver bow tie.

There was also an American on the flight. His name was Leibowitz. He spoke to you in the van after you picked him up from outside The Plaza. It was still dark. He leaned over the front passenger seat and spoke in the slow, easy way that the older Americans sometimes have.

'After my wife passed I decided to strike out on my own and see the world.'

'Good for you.' You were driving slowly. Winter's first ice was on the road.

'This is my seventh country in six months.'

He seemed to you to be about seventy but looked to be in very good shape; lanky and straight-backed in the American tourist's uniform of a Red Sox cap, jeans, and a padded jacket done up against the pre-dawn chill.

That trip also had three locals – Peter Johnstone and his son, Michael, and Michael's friend. It was Michael's eleventh birthday and the flight was a present from his parents. They thought he would have a better time if he had a young friend to share the experience with. You often recall how, in the park, while the huge envelope was filling, Michael and his friend stood closer to the flames than any of the others. The van's headlights illuminated the scene and gave you enough light to work.

'Watch out,' you said. 'Last week a couple of boys lost their eyebrows. Pheew! Gone.'

Michael's friend was a pale redhead. He took a couple of steps back, but Michael stood his ground. 'You're just joking, aren't you,' he said.

'Sure.' And you winked.

The envelope was filling quickly. Everyone watched as it tried to rise, slowly staggering up, like a fat drunkard getting out of bed. It looked like it was going to be a good flight. The sky was clear of clouds and there was no wind yet. The punters seemed to you to be a nice easy group. Still, you were disappointed that you only had six bookings that morning. Another three or four would have been better. But it was mid-week, when the numbers were sometimes down, especially when the ski season was late starting, as it was that year. On the bright side though, Saturday morning's flight was already full.

* * *

You see Mrs Nishiura after the speeches have begun. You have moved closer but remain up in the dunes. She is sitting in the second row, behind the group from the Japanese consulate. Their unshuffling, shiny, black shoes are juxtaposed against the grey sand. The Mayor is well into her speech. You are close enough now to hear the phrase 'bonds of sorrow.' Those three words drift down the beach, almost, but not quite, drowned out by the sound of the waves, and land at your feet.

From this distance Mrs Nishiura is not as beautiful as you remember her. In profile, her chin may be slightly sunken, her shoulders just that little hunched. These are things that you do not recall. Her profile is not visible in the wedding photo that you still look at so often, even though you try not to. You watch her as she sits with her back to the ocean and listens to the Mayor. It is a struggle to reconcile your frequently revisited memories of her with the woman you now see.

Reaching down, you break off a piece of the cascade of ice-plant at your feet. It curves to a point like a soft claw. You have a memory of your mother telling you that the juice from these things helps heal cuts, although you don't remember if she ever applied any to your own childhood wounds. You squeeze hard using your finger and thumb and watch the plant crush and the clear liquid drip down. It makes small dark circles on the sand.

When you look back again Mrs Nishiura is staring directly at you. You look away. It is possible she has not recognised you; that she imagines she is looking at a stranger. Perhaps she is simply wondering why a man would stand still and apart for so long. You know that seven years have changed you. Back then you were a few months off forty, but clinging stubbornly to your youth. Now you are a few months off forty-seven, recently divorced from your long-suffering wife, and between jobs. You have enough insight left to be aware that you now look older than your years.

You thrust your hands into the deep pockets of your hoody and start to slidewalk down the face of the dune. When you get to the beach you keep going towards the ocean, through the fringe of driftwood that marks the high-tide, until you are standing at the very edge of the water. Even though there is still no wind, the waves have picked up since you arrived, and roll in with a loud hiss.

When you up look up the beach Mrs Nishiura has her back to you and is again listening to the Mayor.

* * *

The sun was just cracking the curve of the eastern horizon as you rose above the tops of the plane trees at the edge of the park. At two hundred metres you began your patter. *My Beautiful Balloon Ltd* was one of the few commercial operations in the world lucky enough to take off from the centre of a city. You pointed out the cathedral, of course, and the botanical gardens, the Arts Centre and the new gallery with its walls of glass. The first cars were heading in to the city from the suburbs, their headlights still on.

'Where's he going now?' asked Mr Leibowitz. He pointed over the edge of the basket to where Grant was driving the van out of the park. The van's roof was a white rectangle in the half-light.

'He's going to follow us and pick us up when we land.'

'Is there some type of landing pad?' asked Mr Johnstone. Michael and his friend were listening intently.

'No. It's impossible to say *precisely* where we'll come down. Because we're dependant on the wind to steer, no two flights are exactly the same.'

Johnstone and Leibowitz nodded and went back to taking photographs. The Nishiuras had their heads close together and were speaking to each other in hushed voices. You were unsure how much English they had. Like most Japanese, and you had met a lot, they'd probably studied it at school for years but didn't speak more than a phrase or two.

Michael and his friend moved from one side of the basket to the other, craning their necks to see over the side. You didn't mind. They weren't annoying anyone and there was plenty of room, the basket could take up to eleven.

Only Michael's father seemed nervous. 'You OK, Peter?' you asked. There was nearly always a nervous one.

'Fine, fine, yeah, fine. Well, I've never liked heights that much.' He smiled a crooked smile.

'Don't worry. Statistically speaking this is safer than driving your car to work.'

The bright blue and yellow panels of the balloon were shining in the clear morning light. You turned the valve above your head. Burning propane roared up the throat of the balloon lifting you all higher and higher.

* * *

'Did you check the weather forecast?'

The Air Accidents Inspector was named Morse: Inspector Morse. You would have found that funny under different circumstances. It was the day after, and the inspector was perched on a tall stool next to your hospital bed. You still remember moving your feet around beneath the heavy white sheets, making hills and valleys. That morning's newspaper lay on the metal side-table. Your father had brought the paper in earlier during his stoic visit. Mr and Mrs Nishiura stared up at you from the front page. You had already asked a nurse to bring you some scissors so that you could cut the photograph out.

'Of course I checked.'

He nodded and made a note on the form stuck to the clipboard that he was holding. 'Do you remember what the forecast said?'

'A southerly front was due, but not until midday.'

He nodded again. 'And you didn't consider cancelling the flight?'

'We took off at seven-thirty and were supposed to be on the ground again by nine. There shouldn't have been a problem.'

'I spoke to the driver of your chase vehicle – Mr Turnbull.'

'Grant.'

'Yes. He doesn't remember if you launched a pibal to check the upper wind currents. Did you?'

He asked the question casually, as though there was nothing of significance hanging on the answer, as though he was asking if you had had a cup of coffee with your breakfast that morning. You noticed that his nose was large and fleshy but that his eyes were a very clear blue.

'I think I did,' is what you replied. Morse raised an eyebrow. 'Yes. I'm *sure* I did.'

* * *

Your flights generally caught the easterly flows, which carried the balloon over the western suburbs and into the flat farmland beyond, though sometimes there were southerly or south-westerly currents such as the one you had entered. They tended to be stronger air streams than the easterlies, but well within the balloon's tolerance, and your ability as a pilot, to handle.

You radioed Grant in the van and told him what had happened. You said that you would land in the north-east of the city, closer to the coast, probably in the grounds of the old Commonwealth Games stadium, QE2. You had landed there dozens of times over the three years since you co-founded the company. Grant was unconcerned by the change in plan. He told you he was going to the McDonald's drive-through to get himself some breakfast.

'Just another day at the office,' he said.

'No worries.'

But fifteen minutes later the wind had picked up. There was some dark cumulus coming up over the hills to the south that you didn't like the look off. You pulled on the control line that opened the vent at the top of the envelope and let out some air. The balloon dropped a hundred metres but you could not find a new current. The roads and houses and back gardens were beginning to go by quickly.

You must have looked worried because Mr Leibowitz sidled over to you again. The two boys were excited by the increase in speed. Leibowitz spoke quietly so that the boys didn't hear.

'Is everything all right, Chief?'

'Yes, fine. We might have to bring her down a bit early though, because of this wind.'

'It doesn't feel *that* windy.'

'We're moving along with it so you don't feel it the same as if we were standing still.'

The American nodded sagely. 'I get it. But everything's AOK, right?'

'Just dandy,' you said in your best cowboy drawl.

You remember that he grinned and winked. He moved over, as if to say, 'I'll leave you to it', and said something to the Nishiuras that you didn't catch. They both smiled, and Mr Nishiura said. 'We are hoping.'

You radioed Grant back and told him that you were still thinking you would be able to put down in the grounds of the Commonwealth stadium.

Grant had obviously seen the clouds in the south and he sounded tense. 'You sure? You could maybe try for Linwood Park? It's closer.'

'No, the power lines make it too difficult in a wind like this. I don't want to risk it.'

* * *

'Difficult, but not impossible.' That's what Morse had said to you in the hospital.

'I thought it was safer to try for QE2. It was a judgement call.'

He nodded. 'And how long before you realised that you weren't going to be able to land there, after all?'

'About ten minutes. The storm front came through and we got pushed north-east, towards the coast. It was blowing maybe thirty knots.'

'The meteorological service recorded gusts of up to forty-five.'

'I guess they would know.'

A young nurse went by in the corridor and looked in curiously through the partially open door. Maybe she recognised you from page two of that morning's paper. Your photo was there, taken from the company's brochure, right next to a shot of a balloon in flight – though not one of yours.

Morse flicked over a few pages on his clipboard until he found what he was looking for. 'Am I right in thinking that you and the other two partners were in negotiations to sell *My Beautiful Balloon Limited?*

You frowned. 'Yes.'

'And for the last six months you've been scheduling extra flights so that the company looked profitable.'

'It *was* profitable.'

'*More* profitable, I should say.'

'Yes, that's true.'

'So it wouldn't have been in your interests to cancel any flights.' He leaned forward over your bed so that he was almost above you, looking down.

* * *

You were no longer pretending that everything was all right. The southerly front had come through hard and fast. It brought a sharp drop in temperature and it had begun to rain. The six passengers huddled together near the middle of the basket. No one spoke. They were all watching you and you were watching the altimeter. The houses and the roads flashed by eighty metres beneath you.

'It's okay, everyone. Everything's going to be fine.' You tried to sound like you meant it.

Mr and Mrs Nishiura both blinked slowly. His boyish face was now a mask of bewilderment. She looked very small, diminished by the danger. Mathew's father had pulled his son towards himself so that the boy was standing with his back against his father's chest. His dad's arms were clasped around him. Mathew's friend stood next to them and raised his fist to his mouth and bit his knuckles. He began to cry, but silently.

'Have you ever been in this situation before?' Peter Johnstone asked. His voice was high and shaky, mainly, you imagined, because he was with his son and his son's friend.

'Sure, a few times.'

Actually you had only been caught in a wind this strong once before. It had been years ago, in Australia, before you had your licence, and even then it was in a much smaller balloon and over farmland, not rooftops and power lines. The guy who had taken you up had broken an arm in two places during the landing.

You were over the coastal suburbs now and low enough to make out a woman hurriedly pulling in her washing from the clothesline. She looked up as the balloon passed. You were low enough to see her mouth open wide in surprise, and the white of her teeth. Then she was gone.

'What's the plan, Chief?' A wry smile pulled at the corners of Mr Leibowitz's mouth. You were grateful to him.

'I'm going to put it down on the beach.'

* * *

You are still looking out at the sea when Mrs Nishiura comes and stands next to you.

'The weather is beautiful today,' she says. She speaks the words slowly as if they have been memorised from a textbook. Over her shoulder you see that the commemoration ceremony is finished. The Mayor and the group from the consulate have disappeared back over the dunes. The reporters and other guests have broken into small groups and are scattering along the beach, heading back to their cars. The woman in the suit is beginning to pack away the chairs.

'I have never heard you speak English. You speak very well.' You say it because you can think of nothing else to say to her, and because it is close to being true.

She smiles and shakes her head. 'I go to lessons in Sapporo. My teacher is also Kiwi. Called Jo.'

You nod and look back out to sea. She turns her head and follows your gaze. The balloon, having overshot the beach, crashed a hundred and fifty metres out from where you are now standing. In his official report, Morse estimated that you were travelling at between thirty and thirty-five kilometres an hour when the basket hit the water.

Again you hear the sound of the wicker snapping and remember the feeling of the basket lurching violently sideways, pulled by the partially inflated envelope. Winter's shockingly cold seawater surged in. Screaming. Shouts. Foaming water. Crying. When everything settled down a little, you saw that Mr Leibowitz had a streaming gash over his eye, but that he was helping Michael's friend hang on to the mostly submerged basket, which sloshed up and down in the large swell. There were tangled ropes everywhere. It was dim and raining and the sea was choppy, although you were, thank God, out beyond the big breakers. You could also see Johnstone and his son. They were clinging to the far side of the basket from where you were. You could hear a woman crying but did not know where the noise was coming from. There was blood in the water around you and it took you a long time, or what seemed to be a long time, to work out that it was yours.

Finally two terrified surfers were there. They were shouting and one of them was pulling you onto her board. You felt her slick black wetsuit against your face. She said something about your leg and it was then that you saw the rip in your trousers and the exposed meat beneath, but there wasn't any pain. Lying over the rough fibreglass board you could still hear a woman crying. You couldn't imagine who it was. That is the last thing that you remember before the ambulance.

'Are you still … pilot?' Mrs Nishiura asks and looks up at the moon.

'No. I've had a lot of jobs lately. For a while I sold real estate.' She does not understand, and you explain the job to her in simple words.

She smiles and nods. 'We have in Japan also.'

'What do you do?' you ask.

'I marry again. My husband is teacher. I have two children and look after.'

You have not really looked at her since she approached you. Now you turn to her. She is not a frail fairy, and she is not tragic, as you have always imagined her to be. She is not even particularly beautiful. Here on the beach, free from the amber of your memory, she is just a normal looking Japanese woman with passable English, who is standing on the edge of the ocean. She is simply a woman who was once unlucky enough to have married a man who never learned to swim.

It is suddenly clear to you that her life has moved on in the last seven years. She is not even Mrs Nishiura any more. You do not even know her name. You turn away and, although it is not that cold, you begin to shake uncontrollably. You push your hands deep into your pockets and hope that she will not notice. Neither of you speak for a long time.

'The chairs,' you say, at last. 'They should have been facing the ocean.'

'Yes. I think so too.'

She turns quickly and walks back up the beach. For a moment you think that she is leaving, that she is tired of you. You don't blame her. But then you see that she has stopped up by the SUV and is speaking to the woman whose job it now is to put away the chairs.

When she begins to walk back towards you she is carrying three folded chairs, which she holds cradled over her arm. She is small, and carrying the chairs on the sand is a struggle. You walk up the beach to meet her and help carry two of the chairs back to where you had both been standing.

You watch as she unfolds each chair and places it carefully, until there is a perfect line of chairs a short distance beyond where the waves push up the beach, darkening the sand. She sits on one end of the short row. You hesitate, and then you join her. Between you is an empty chair. Above the ocean the pale moon is low in the sky. You sit like that for a long time, contemplating the sea, and the sky, and everything in between.

All the Soul-and-Body Scars

Sarah Weir

Without realising it, I find that I've stopped the car in the middle of the track. This is harder than I thought. I take a deep breath and stare out of the window. The bush is darkly silent. Hardly a bird call, just leaves brushing against each other. Only a few metres in, there are plants that have never experienced direct light, that grow only in the hope of it.

Why didn't I come later? After five, once he's opened the bar. Liquored up he is ebullient, lyrical and, though I don't like to admit it, easier. Then we rave on about poetry, philosophy, metaphysics and quantum physics. Last time he told me all about the tenth dimension. Quantum physics, he said, is a process of deduction; take the tenth dimension. No-one has ever seen it, we can only conclude from the evidence we have that it must exist. Rather like the way the rest of the world must seem to a fish underwater, vaguely aware of movement and light flickering above the surface and sensing something else, some other world out there but never able to see it.

It would be easy to come after five, yet something stubborn and perverse stops me, as if I am still searching for the real him, as if he still exists in a fleeting fragment of time; after the hang-over, the early morning crankiness, the reek of ketones has worn off his skin and before the onset of the first drink. I don't know why I bother. During the afternoon he is terse and uncommunicative. There are fractious silences through which I extract reluctant conversation while he waits for the hands of the clock to move forward.

This time it will be worse. It has been six weeks since we've heard from him. I don't know what kind of state he's going to be in. I'm half expecting a skeleton propped up on the porch.

I start the car again. The last part of the track is a steep incline full of potholes and greasy mud. Once over the brow of the hill, the bush abruptly fades and I drive through a bank of toi toi, their feathery heads bent forwards from the offshore wind.

As I pull up to the bach, I see that time has become irrelevant anyway. He's sitting on the porch staring out to sea in bare feet and an old jacket, a half drunk bottle of beer by his side. I walk towards him. His white hair is flattened by the wind.

'She's sent the search parties I see,' he says, swigging from the bottle. 'Didn't I sign out properly?'

Immediately, I'm back in the web, caught between the two of them.

'Jesus,' I say, already furious. 'I'm not a fucking war correspondent. Ring her yourself if you want to insult her.'

'So, what did she send? Vitamins, fibre, new-age remedies, home-made soup …'

'I bought them,' I snap, turning towards the car, keys in hand and almost ready to jump back in, 'so I don't have to eat the shit you live on.'

We are used to his casual disappearances to the holiday bach. Two, three weeks of solitude to work on an article or a lecture. Or just to think.

And then lately, to drink. We have learned not to pay too much attention to his absences, the less we say about them the more likely he is to return. Only this time he hasn't come back.

Carrying the food boxes into the kitchen, the familiar damp-sweet bach smell conjures a mirage of sun-soaked memories. Through the window, I catch him leaning forward in his chair scratching his leg. His neck has shrunk. The veins almost hang loose as he bends forward. It has happened so quickly. His wrists are dwarfed by his shirt cuffs, a spindly bone juts through his yellowed skin. The old marbled linoleum starts to swim before me, like a shoal of fish darting this way and that. I grasp hold of a chair to steady myself, then pull out the bottle of Jim Beam.

'When did you last eat anyway?' I ask, walking back out to the deck and pouring us both a large, neat whiskey in the scratched cut glass tumblers that pre-date even the bach.

'I had some soup …' he says vaguely.

'For God's sake Dad …' He looks up at me, his shrunken face bristling with whitened stubble, his eyes wrinkled helplessly and he shrugs. 'Don't worry. I brought stuff,' I say, swallowing the whiskey back, waiting for the relief to hit.

The bach is built on a cliff. We sit in silence and stare out at the mercurial ocean. The rocky beach down below is accessible only by a rickety rope ladder, for those who have the stomach for it.

'What have you been doing?' I ask.

'Sitting here mainly.'

'You been alright?'

'Word I was in the house alone / Somehow must have gotten abroad / Word I was in my life alone / Word I had no one left but God,' he said, quoting Robert Frost, his favourite poet.

'What happened to five o'clock?'

He turns away. 'Waiting just seemed pointless,' he says.

My love for him comes in these brief, choking moments, like a heart attack, then dies as quickly as it came.

'How's Ray?' he asks.

'Ray left,' I say, pouring us another whiskey. 'I'm too difficult, apparently.'

'You're too like me.'

'I still wait until five.'

'Aargh well, that's something, I suppose.' A black cloud sweeps towards us from the sea.

'Southerly's blowing in,' he comments.

We have always communicated through poetry. It is a ritual which establishes our connection, as we speak through the words and ideas of others far better equipped to communicate than each of us. We rarely talk about us, how, who or what we are.

There is a timelessness out here on the deck. During thunderstorms he'd sit us on the old ripped armchair, springs hanging out of the back, jiggling on his knee, while forks of lightning raced through the ionized air and thunder cracked the cliff tops. No matter how close the lightning came, he never suggested a retreat. Nature is beautiful, but random, he would say. Completely unpredictable. Don't ever think it's personal, it's completely ignorant of our existence. You can deal with anything, once you realise how random it all is.

But his words had the opposite effect and their utterance always filled me with an inexplicable terror. It was like he introduced us to his own chaos, too early, before we were ready for it.

In the fridge there is only half a carton of milk, an opened can of beans and some cheese. I check the fireplace. There are no signs of ash or charcoal, no firewood or kindling in the basket. His rod is propped up behind the door, with a tangled line lying beside it. Has he moved off that armchair at all? I start chopping vegetables for dinner, then put the onion down and storm out, kitchen knife still in my hand.

'Have you just given up?' I demand.

He doesn't answer.

'Damn you.' I storm back inside, slamming the sliding door. I don't know why I'm bothering. Tears stream helplessly as I double up against the bench, holding on to it, before sinking to my knees. He's already cutting ties, slipping away. I'm trying to hold on to him but there's nothing to hold on to, nothing at all. I've been taking mental snapshots, trying to capture some image that will remain with me. The back of his head, staring impassively out to sea, the once fretful fingers now still around his glass. You can remember images and you can remember what it feels like to be around people. I don't want to remember this feeling. I had something far more sentimental in mind.

While the chicken is simmering, I go outside and chop some firewood. There is kindling, I discover, in the shed.

I am surprised when he leaves his chair and comes inside for dinner. He takes tiny mouthfuls, like a famine victim, swallowing gingerly. The winter sun dips below the ocean rim. He asks how everyone is. We crack jokes about my brother Reuben's latest New Age philosophies and he asks me about my work.

'Are you in pain?'

'Sometimes,' he says. 'But I'm not usually sober enough to notice.'

He eats half before giving up. Not before telling me over and over again how nice it is and how much he appreciates it. It is dark by the time we go back outside, with our blankets and coffee and the remains of the whiskey.

'So, what's the plan?' The question spills out. I didn't know I was going to ask him this. 'You just going to stay here until it's all over?'

He shrugs. 'I don't have a plan,' he says. 'I needed to come here. I don't know why.' His left hand shakes as he picks up his coffee.

'And what about us?' I continue. 'What are we supposed to do while you escape to the wilderness? It's like you've already died. Mum is quietly going hysterical.'

'She wants to talk about it,' he says, with sudden anguish. 'And I ... I can't.'

'You've always been like this,' I say. 'You could never talk about things.'

'Far in the pillared dark / Thrush music went – / Almost like a call to come in / To the dark and lament / But no, I was out for the stars / I would not come in./ I meant, not even if asked/ And I hadn't been.' He quoted in his lyrical voice, then added quietly, 'I'm still out for the stars. I'm not ready for the dark.' I have no answer for this. I am not ready either.

'None of it makes any sense, he says. 'Nothing of what I've done. Nothing of what is happening. It's always been pointless.'

After a certain amount of whiskey he always gets sentimental; then the melancholic despair sets in. It tears at something inside of me and I remember what it feels like to fall without being caught. Suddenly I'm yelling, screaming, things I've been yelling at him for years in my head.

'Do you realise what that did to us as kids? Hearing over and over how everything was pointless. Didn't you realise what you were saying. That we were pointless, that our existence had no meaning. You're always poking fun at Reuben for his relentless New Age positivity, but for God's sake, he's got no sense of meaning ... you stripped it all away.'

'Any sense of meaning is merely ... an artificial construct ... an illusion ...'

'Parents are supposed to protect their children from chaos, not teach it to them. Kids need twigs.'

'You just need to be able to think things through.'

'It's not enough and you know it. There's no point in being able to think about things if you're drowning in chaos. The finest analytic mind needs roots, something to hold it down.'

'Oh Jesus,' he says … 'if that's what you were hoping for …'

'It's not so much to ask. We just wanted to matter to you.'

'You've got it all wrong,' he sighs.

'I am filled with tripwires that constantly blow. Nothing is stable. Nothing.'

'Oh grow up.' He staggers up off the armchair, swaying. 'Stop blaming me for everything. I didn't drive Ray away. You taught yourself to be an obnoxious bitch.'

'It was the you in me he couldn't stand.' I've spent my whole life waiting for this fight.

Practising, rehearsing with others. He has to know the extent of his incompetence.

Now it's actually happening, I can't go through with it.

I don't want him to die thinking he's failed. I just want him to say he's always loved me. Which is stupid, because I know he did. I just never felt it which is a different thing altogether and I don't know what he'd have to do for me to feel that.

No wonder Ray left.

When I open my eyes, Dad has disappeared. He's not inside, not in the shed … he must have … Oh… no. I run inside for a torch. Standing at the top of the cliff, I shine my torch down. His whitened face and shrunken eyes flare up at me from the rope ladder.

'What are you doing Dad?'

'Getting away.'

'You're too drunk Dad … come back up …'

He climbs down another couple of rungs.

'Stop. For God's sake. Come back up … please Dad.'

There is a silence. When I shine the torch he blinks at me, his fingers gripping like withered claws.

Then he says, in a thin voice 'I can't ... can't make it back up.'

The night spins in front of me. Just like the night a couple of months ago, when he got knocked down by a motorbike as he was staggering back from the bottle store. He wasn't badly hurt, just bruised his ribs, but I took him to the hospital anyway to get an x-ray. The doctor returned with a strange look. Dad's ribs were fine he said, but there were a few anomalies on the x-ray they'd like to check out further. A medical understatement and a half. The cancer had already spread to his liver.

'Thought I'd been losing weight,' he said impassively.

Then later, back at their place. 'Just one random event. That's all it takes.'

It wasn't long after that that he disappeared. Without saying a word about it to any of us.

'Hold on,' I yell.

'I'm going to fall,' he says. 'Under the circumstances, it's the most sensible option.' His words are slurred.

'Don't be so selfish.'

The ladder has never been able to withstand more than one person and even if I risk it, I'll never be able to bring him back up by myself. I peer down at the sea. It is high tide and the water is within metres of the cliff. At low tide you can walk back down to the road.

'Climb down to the beach. I'll follow and wait there with you.'

My mind is reeling, I keep thinking there is something I should be doing, but I can't think of it, I'm way too drunk. My thoughts are sliding into one another. I shine the torch to guide his hands and he climbs down gingerly. When he is almost at the bottom he calls up to me.

'Hey.'

'What?'

'Bring some coffee.'

I climb down with a backpack filled with old army blankets and a flask of coffee. Still, neither buffers us from the wind. We watch the black water, folding over itself against the rocks, white mouthed in the moonlight. The cold sets in. It will be several hours before the tide will be low enough to walk out.

I feel his elbow and shoulder touching mine as we lean against a rock, wrapped in blankets. We haven't been this close in a long time. My eyelids close, the night sways, the sea shushes in my ears as it washes through the kelp. As my head nods, I hear him muttering. 'A voice said, look me in the stars / And tell me truly, men of earth / If all the soul-and-body scars / Were not too much to pay for birth.' Then he adds, 'Frost never quite entered the darkness though. He felt its invitation, but never went close enough to enter it. Eminently sensible. Not like Eliot who went right in.'

He is trying to express his love. But it exists in a fourth, fifth or tenth dimension. By now my teeth are chattering. I lean closer to him. He is shaking too. Alcohol has blinded me to the precariousness of our position. What if he is not strong enough to endure the cold? How frail is he? What if he doesn't last the night? I force my eyes open and peer into the wind, the black sea a blur.

'I knew this would happen,' he says, tipping the last of the coffee into a cup.

'What?'

'All this unfinished business. I knew you'd all want to relieve yourselves of it before I go.'

'Is that why you ran away?

'No. But I wanted to be up to it when I got back. Improve on past performances, so to speak.'

'What shall we do? Shall I ring for help, get more blankets ..?'

'Oh, don't bother,' he says vaguely. 'I'm about ready to climb back up ...'

'But.'

'Oh God,' he laughs, 'I'm not … I was just too drunk. That old ladder sways too much, arms like jelly. I often have to wait down here before sobering up.'

He heaves himself back up, shaking the pins and needles from his legs, putting the empty flask in his jacket pocket.

'I just thought it would be nice, you know, to sit here …'

'Oh.'

'It was, wasn't it?'

I nod, feeling like a fish when a face peers into the water from overhead and the opaque features refract across the ceiling of the fish's world, which instantly darkens as the overhanging flesh dances and bends in the ripples. By swimming closer I can glimpse a tantalising hint of a vast otherness, a whole world, that I have yearned to grasp, to believe in. Always wanting to believe that there is more to him than what I see.

These are the snapshots that I must collect. These rare glimpses, usually during alcoholic moments where a door opens to a fleeting understanding. They will be superimposed onto the physical images, the sight of him nimbly shinnying up the ladder, his jacket flapping, his withered hands grasping the rungs and standing up above me, saying, 'I think there's another bottle somewhere, what do you think?'

Castles in the Sand

Nicola Kimpton

His eyes are restless like the waves. From beneath the shade of the pohutukawa, Cam scans the golden strip of coastline stretching out towards the rugged East Cape hills. The sand shifts under the weight of the Saturday morning crowd as new arrivals fan out over the beach, claiming their piece of paradise for the day.

In the car park, vehicles fight for spaces like greedy seagulls over scraps, while the sun shines sharp on sunbathers lying still like stones on the sand. An orchestra of cicadas scrape out their song in the tree above – their rhythm intensifies, competing with the thump of a stereo from a nearby car.

Out by the sea, Jack sculpts sand between his fingers. Like a potter at his wheel, his eyes, blue like his mother's, are focused in concentration. He looks up, catches Cam's eye, smiles.

'I'm gonna build big a castle, Dad – for you and Mum.' That was Jack's promise to them as they arrived at the beach.

'Sounds great,' Cam had said, envying his youthful resolve.

In the chair beside him, Tania flicks through a magazine. The pink halter neck bikini adds a vivid contrast to her pale skin. Her dark blonde hair is combed back off her face, her wraparounds shield her eyes from intrusion. The plastic deck chairs keep them at a comfortable distance; the chilly bin breaches the gap with its cool, impartial presence.

Cam opens his mouth to say something, closes it. He sighs; flips open his book, a historical novel – somewhere safe to retreat. He tries to concentrate, but the words blur; transient, fluid, out of reach. Like Tania.

They met here, ten years ago at Ohope Beach. Labour Weekend, and Cam, a surf lifeguard, watched boogie boarders, swimmers and surfers surge and spill on the waves. His first glimpse of Tania had been her golden hair, streaked out over the water. A closer look revealed those slim, pale arms clutching at air. He'd thrashed through the waves, pounding the water to reach her.

'My knight in shining togs,' she'd called him as she recovered on the sand.

He'd laughed – with relief, and something deeper. He'd saved her life; changed his own in the process.

The car stereo's cranked up and sand sprays Cam's toes as two teenage boys race past him. A pair of teenage girls chase after them, whipping their towels at the boys' legs. Cam watches as they collapse onto the sand, wrestling and ticking each other. Their laughter spirals into the air, mixes with the beat of the stereo in a heady concoction.

Cam glances across at Tania, wonders what she's thinking. She holds the pages of her magazine taut, her tinted lips tight, unreadable.

Cam licks his lips; they're dry in the heat. It had been his idea to come here again. 'Let's drive out to the coast, have a couple of beers, relax in the sun,' he'd said. She'd given him that blank look of hers; distanced, remote as if she wasn't really there.

'It'll be good for Jack,' he'd added. Like it required justification.

She'd relented and so here they were, playing happy families at the beach.

He reaches into the chilly bin. A cool blast of air sucks the heat from his fingers. He grasps the neck of the bottle and prises it open. Offers it to Tania.

'Beer?'

The magazine twitches slightly. 'Okay.'

Their fingers brush as the bottle passes between them. He could have put a message in it. But he wouldn't know what to write, what to say. He never does.

'Thanks.' Her tone flat, hushed.

She takes a long, deep draught and lifts her gaze to the beach where Jack's careful fingers mould his masterpiece. The castle climbs steadily higher. He looks up from his creation to smile at them both. Pauses, uncertain.

Cam moves his gaze to a group of kids scouring the shoreline for shells. He feels like an empty shell; curled in on himself, hollow. He replays his conversation with Tania in bed last night, trying to 'work through their issues' as the counsellor had suggested. Batting words from opposite sides of the mattress, the heated volley cut short by Tania's deluge of words.

'Things happened too fast...I didn't want to be tied down...Jack is great but...'

But.

She'd taken a deep breath. 'I don't think this is working anymore.'

He'd heard those words before, in movies and books, seen couples fall apart – wondered how they never saw it coming.

Now he knew.

A squeal draws Cam's attention back to the beach. The teens continue to roll and tumble in the sand. The beach pulses with their energy. Cam recalls the first soft surprise of Tania's naked skin, as they flirted in the dunes; hungry, eager, naïve. Careless.

Tania removes suntan lotion from her bag. The cicadas up tempo. A humming, chirping drumroll. The ocean roars in Cam's ears.

'Here, let me...' he says. His words sound strange, unfamiliar.

Tania pauses. All around them, the teen's laughter bubbles and froths. She clasps the lotion as if unable to let go.

'All right.' She passes the lotion to Cam and leans forward slowly. The imprint of the deck chair traces delicate patterns over her back.

Cam pours lotion onto his hands. It oozes over his fingers, the sticky sweet smell of coconut scents the air. He smoothes a thin layer of lotion over Tania's shoulders.

She flinches slightly – at the touch or the coolness, he's unsure which.

He makes small circles with his fingers. Traces the imprints on her back, works his way up towards her shoulders.

Paints soft, smooth strokes over her skin.

Time stops. The squeals, the roar of the ocean, the stereo – everything fades into the background. Only the cicadas continue with a gentle, acoustic hum.

'That feels good.' Tania's words barely a whisper. As ethereal and surprising as her 'yes' to his marriage proposal, the summer they'd found out about Jack. That night on the beach with the waves curling around them, Cam had believed that together they'd be all right.

Tania relaxes her shoulders, leans in to his touch. He runs his fingers over the soft curve of her neck, breaching the invisible distance between them with his hands. He's afraid to stop, to lose this unusual closeness, this connection.

Tania turns around slowly.

She lowers her sunglasses to look at him. Her eyes, a deep flash of blue reflecting the ocean.

Cam's heart pulses. His eyes connect with hers. Searching, trying to reach her.

There's a sudden pounding of feet over the sand.

'Mum! Dad! My sandcastle – it's ruined! The waves got it!'

For a moment, they stay still. Then, the moment fractures, the sand shifts.

Jack stands before them, his hands curled in frustration. Tears streak his sandy cheeks.

Tania's eyes turn grey, the sunglasses snap back into place. She folds her arms around Jack, protectively, instinctively.

'Don't worry, son,' Cam hears himself saying. Like he can bring it back. Like he can bring her back.

His gaze expands to a wider focus. The teens have moved further down the beach, searching for new territory. The thump of the stereo amplifies, drowning out the cicadas.

Jack slumps at their feet, curls his arms around Tania's legs.

They stare out at the water, watching the waves roll over the castle, shaping the sand into something new.

Reading the Waves

Jackie Davis

That Taranaki summer was short. It arrived swiftly, like a prickly rash, taking over everything. Lawns burned and shrivelled. The tar melted on the wide asphalt streets. Runny liquorice in the gutters. Tomatoes warm from the garden, skins smooth and tight. Barbeques on the back lawn, the shrill of cicadas. Make the most of it, Mum said. It'll be over soon.

Every afternoon that summer, I sat at the window and waited until Dad came home from work. Each day trawled past slowly. I ached and itched with the sluggishness of it. And now here was Dad, coming up the driveway waving madly to me. Hello love, as he got out of his car. How was your day? Hello dear, to Mum, and kissing her on her pink evening lips.

Who's for a swim at the beach then?

Me, me, an eager puppy scampering at his feet. All right, togs on and I'll race you to the car.

Ready? Towels rolled into tubes, jandals, a yellow flutter board.

Ready.

Strandon beach was Dad's favourite. Family friendly, he called it. We dashed across the hot sand, racing to lay our towels down, our feet finding relief on the knobbly fabric after the burning of the black iron sand. Sometimes I took a magnet to the beach. I'd hold it just above the sand and watch tiny fragments of iron jump from the beach onto the surface of the magnet. Clinging onto each other like circus gymnasts.

Dad was teaching me how to body surf. Watch me, he said, and he'd swim out to where the waves first took hold. You've got to read the waves, he shouted. His voice was buffeted in on the surf, falling before me, ankle deep in the water. Start in before they break. Then the wave will pick you up. You'll have to kick and kick and you'll feel the wave lift you and it'll be as though it's carrying you. Make yourself as long as possible. You're an arrow, a spear, a comet shooting through the sky.

Watch me, and he found the wave, at the moment when it was breathy and full of waiting. It was as though he'd been catching waves his whole life. It scooped him up, that wave, and he allowed it to, giving in to it and he was as sleek as a fish, fingertips stretched, toes pointing, taller now than any man.

See? he said and he skimmed in next to me. Your turn.

I followed him out, into the sea, the wide, wild Tasman. Gripping onto my yellow flutter board, digging my fingertips into it. I tried to stand in his footfalls because the sea bed slid and slurried under my feet and I was afraid it might disappear underneath me completely. Up to my hips, my waist, my meagre chest. Stopping to let the waves past, not pushing up against them, but giving them the right of way.

Right. This is the spot, Dad said. He turned around to face the shore. It might have been a mile away. He turned his back to the waves that were ready to break behind him. My fearless father.

Are you ready?

Nodding. My eyes stinging, the sound of the sea inside my head.

All around me.

Read the waves. One two three go.

I threw myself forward, buoyant and bouncing on the water, my flutter board pointing me in. Nothing happened. The wave slid over me, slippery and thick and I watched it break and crash in front of me.

Never mind. Try again.

So I did. Again and again. Disappointed to be left behind by the waves so many times. I'll never get it, I thought. I wanted to cry.

One more. This time, love.

Reading the wave again, kicking off, fingers deep in the foamy edge of the flutter board. This time.

Yes, yes, Dad's voice all around me. It had me, the wave. I was keeping up with it. I was long and smooth, on top of the water, defying gravity and sense and fear and I streaked in, salty water spraying off my face. Not daring to breathe. The sensation lasting forever. This ride. Not seeing anything, not my fingertips white against the board, not the froth of the wave, not the beach rushing towards me.

Then slowing. Feeling the wave lose strength. Its momentum slipping away. I skidded across the shallow water. It was warm and the sand was black underneath. Coming to rest there, the end of the wave. It sliding past me as it was sucked back out.

And Dad was there, his hand huge on my back. You did it, you did it. Well done.

Finding my breath somewhere inside me. And standing up and my legs trembling with effort and the excitement and the realisation.

Do you want to go again?

No thanks, I said and my hand found my father's. Let's go home.

And now I find myself back at a beach. At the edge of the land again. Poverty Bay now. Here the sand is pale. Less intense. Sunsets are yellower.

The sea is the colour of paua, shimmering, iridescent.

Read the waves, I call to my son. Start in before they break, see? I catch one, I'm kicking, pointing my toes. My fingers are long, stretching. I am weightless again, the wave is carrying me in. I am wrapped in it. The ride of my life.

Your turn, I say as I skim in next to my son.

This is the spot. Read the waves.

And as I teach my child, it is my father's voice that pitches across the surface of the sea to him. It is carried by the wind, the foamy surf. It is my father reaching out to us both.

My son finds a wave, His small body kicks and he catches it. He is as sleek as a fish. He is gone from me.

I watch him let the sea take him in. You've done it, I shout. I skip through the shallows where the water is warm, to my son, gasping, smiling, his fingers hard against his bodyboard. My hand is large on his back. Well done, I say. He looks up at me, his face shining, dripping. His smile is as wide as the Pacific.

I want to say to him, try again, have another go. But instead I reach for his hand. Come on, I say, and we walk up the beach together. Let's go home.

Contributors

Kath Beattie

Born in Takapuna, Kath spent most of her childhood on a farm at Port Charles, on the Coromandel peninsula. She boarded at Epsom Girls' Grammar School, attended Teachers' Training College at Ardmore, Auckland, taught in New Zealand and overseas, later gaining a Social Science degree from Victoria University of Wellington and working as a social worker until her retirement. Kath has published many short stories, poems and children's readers. Her latest publication is 'Walking Backwards Into Your Future – coping with grief through continuing bonds'. Her favourite beach remains Sandy Bay, near Port Charles, where she first developed a love of the sea, mountains and bush.

David Lyndon Brown

A short story writer and poet, as a young man David was also a champion figure-skater. At the age of fourteen he held three national figure-skating titles and was fifth in the world championships. In 2001 he published his first book of short stories, *Calling the Fish & Other Stories* (University of Otago Press), from which 'Why I Never Learned to Swim' is taken. In 2007 Titus Books published his 'crepuscular' novella, *Marked Men*, and a collection of David's poetry, *Skin Hunger*, will also be published by

Titus Books. David lives in Auckland and his favourite beach is Martins Bay, near Leigh.

Jackie Davis

Jackie Davis was born in New Plymouth and spent much of her childhood on the black sand of Strandon and Fitzroy beaches of that city. A Registered Nurse who holds an MA in Creative Writing, her published work ranges from a seventeen syllable haiku to two novels for adults, *Breathe* and *Swim*. She now lives in Gisborne, again on the edge of the land. In 2006 she was the recipient of the New Zealand Society of Authors Foxton Writer's Fellowship, and during her tenure she rekindled her relationship with those wild West Coast beaches. Jackie knows that the sea is such a powerful influence in her life that she will always have to live somewhere 'where the air is tinged with salt and the roar of the sea is in my ears'.

Adrienne Frater

Adrienne was born in Wanganui and after living in many different places in New Zealand, settled in Nelson, where she teaches writing. Since childhood her summers have been spent by the sea or on it. A keen sailor and traveller, she has been fortunate to explore many beaches in various places in the world, and these tend to appear in her writing. She writes both for children and for adults and particularly enjoys radio writing. In 2005 Adrienne's story 'The Words Never Said', was chosen to represent New Zealand in the David K. Wong (PEN International) competition. A beach she returns to frequently is Bark Bay, in the Abel Tasman National Park, where at high tide, 'I can launch myself from the golden sandbank into the turquoise lagoon'.

James George

Novelist and short story writer James George is of Ngapuhi, English and Irish descent. Born in Wellington and now living in Auckland, he calls Northland his 'spiritual home'. His novels are *Wooden Horses, Hummingbird* and *Ocean Roads*. The last two were finalists in the Montana New Zealand Book Awards, *Hummingbird* was also short-listed for the 2005 Tasmania Pacific Fiction Prize and *Ocean Roads* was a finalist in the 2007 Commonwealth Writers' Prize. In 2007 James was the holder of the Buddle Findlay Sargeson Literary Fellowship, during which time he worked on his fourth novel. His favourite beach is Hukatere, on the west coast of Northland.

Alice Glenday

Alice (1920-2004) was born in Ontario, Canada, and came to New Zealand when she was 27. She lived mostly in Palmerston North, where she wrote many short stories, several plays and two novels. Her story 'One Fine Day' won the Katherine Mansfield Short Story Award in 1969. Her first novel, *Follow, Follow*, won the 1973 Auckland City Centennial Fiction Contest. 'A Summer Thing', taken from her second novel *A Population of One* (1991), won the 1990 Mobil Dominion Sunday Times Short Story Award. Alice enjoyed reading, gardening and the theatre. Himatangi on the Manawatu coast was her favourite beach. She loved its ever-changing seashore and sand dunes, and its perennial terns.

Patricia Grace

Born and raised in Wellington, Patricia is a leading New Zealand writer of novels, short stories and children's books. Her work includes the novels *Potiki, Cousins, Dogside Story* and *Tu*, the short story collections *Waiariki* and *The Sky People* and the children's book *The Kuia and the Spider/ Te Kuia me te Pungawerewere*. She has received many awards for her books, and has a DCNZM, QSO for Services to Literature. Patricia lives in Plimmerton, near Wellington, where her favourite beach is, 'the very stony and rugged Hongoeka Bay. I like to walk there, swim there, fish and gather paua there. It's a safe place for little children to play and swim, and where older family members can surf when the wind's up. I enjoy watching the stingrays searching about in the weed, especially in the late afternoons'.

Charlotte Grimshaw

Charlotte was born, raised and educated in Auckland, where she still lives. She is the author of three novels, *Provocation, Guilt* and *Foreign City*, and a collection of short stories, *Opportunity*, which was short-listed for the 2007 International Frank O'Connor Prize and won the Montana Medal for Fiction at the Montana New Zealand Book Awards in 2008. She has twice been a finalist and prize-winner in the *Sunday Star-Times* Short Story Competition and in 2006 won the Katherine Mansfield Short Story Award. Her short stories have appeared in *The Six Pack, The Best New Zealand Fiction* volumes 2, 3, 4 and 5, and in the UK, *Stand* magazine. Her favourite New Zealand beaches are Karekare, on Auckland's west coast, and Whatuwhiwhi, on the Karikari peninsula in the Far North.

David Hill

David was born and grew up in Hawkes Bay and now lives in New Plymouth. A former teacher, he has been a full-time writer since 1983. He writes fiction and non-fiction for adults and (especially) for children, His stories and novels have now been published in seven languages and in New Zealand he has been awarded the Esther Glen Medal, the New Zealand Post Children's Honour Prize and the Margaret Mahy Medal. David also devotes varying amounts of his spare time to archery and astronomy. His favourite beach is a long curve of gritty sand at a bend of the Tutaekuri River in Hawkes Bay, where he learned to swim. He is ashamed to admit that he doesn't much like sea beaches.

Tania Hutley

Tania was born in Auckland and studied English at the University of Auckland. She writes for both adults and children. Her novel for 8 to 12-year-olds will be published by Scholastic early in 2009. Her short stories for adults have been short-listed for the Katherine Mansfield Short Story Award, the *Sunday Star-Times* Short Story Competition and the Royal Society of New Zealand Manhire Prize for Creative Science Writing. In 2006 she won a mentorship through the New Zealand Society of Authors and was mentored by Norman Bilbrough. Her interests include reading, walking, tennis and pilates. Her favourite beach is at Tawharanui Regional Park, where she enjoys picnicking in that romantic setting.

Kevin Ireland

Kevin was born in Mt Albert, Auckland and grew up close to the beaches at Narrow Neck, then Takapuna, on the city's North Shore. After living in London for twenty-five years he returned to live in Devonport, again on 'the Shore'. His many publication include two volumes of memoirs, a collection of short stories, a booklet entitled *On Getting Old* and a discursive book about fishing, *How to Catch a Fish*. Among the many literary honours he has received is the Prime Minister's Award for Poetry, in 2004. His latest books are his seventeenth collection of poems, *How to Survive the Morning* and his fifth novel, *The Jigsaw Chronicles*, both published in 2008 by Cape Catley. Kevin's favourite beach is Cheltenham, near Devonport, 'because it's shallow, safe and just down the road'.

Christine Johnstone

Christine was born and grew up in Dunedin. After studying at the University of Otago she lived with her husband and daughters in England and Germany, then worked as a teacher. Her books include a novel, *Blessed Art Thou Among Women*, which won the Reed Fiction Award in 1990, a short story collection, *The End of the Century* (1999) and another novel, *The Shark Bell* (2002). In 1994 she was the Robert Burns Fellow at the University of Otago. Her short stories have appeared in *Sport* and *Landfall* and have been broadcast by Radio New Zealand. Her favourite beach is St Clair in Dunedin, which inspired her novel *The Shark Bell* and where '... surfers venture out all year... and walkers and runners abound'. Christine lives beside the Otago Harbour.

Nicola Kimpton

Nicola was born in Nottingham, England, and has a BA (Hons) in English from Loughborough University. After moving to New Zealand in 2005 she began writing in earnest and in 2007 was the inaugural recipient of the Kingi McKinnon Scholarship for Emerging Writers. In the same year she was also a prize-winner in the Whakatane Short Story Competition. Her published work includes poems published in the anthology *Tiny Gaps* (2006) and feature articles in *Healthy Options* and *Fitness Life* magazines. Her favourite beach is Ohope, in the Bay of Plenty, where she currently lives and writes. A keen walker, she loves that beach's, 'relaxed atmosphere and stunning views out to the East Cape'.

Graeme Lay

Graeme grew up in coastal Taranaki, beside Oakura and Opunake beaches. There he learned to swim, fish and surf. After graduating from Victoria University of Wellington he lived in England for some years, returning to live on Auckland's North Shore in the early 1970s, where he began writing, publishing first short stories and later, novels for adults and young adults and collections of travel writing. His recent books include the adult novel *Alice & Luigi*, the travel book *Inside the Cannibal Pot* and *In Search of Paradise*, a non-fiction work about the colonial era artists and writers who were inspired by the islands of the South Pacific. Graeme's favourite beach is Narrow Neck, on the North Shore, where he walks, swims and launches his fishing dinghy.

Owen Marshall

Owen was born in Te Kuiti, but spent most of his boyhood in Blenheim and Timaru. He was educated at Timaru Boys' High and the University of Canterbury, graduating with MA (Hons). A novelist as well as a short story writer, his books include the novel *Harlequin Rex*, winner of the Montana New Zealand Book Awards for Fiction in 2000, and *Watch of Gryphons*, which was short-listed for the same prize in 2006. In 2000 he received the ONZM for services to New Zealand Literature, and in 2005 was appointed an adjunct professor at the University of Canterbury. He has held literary fellowships at the universities of Otago and Canterbury, and the Katherine Mansfield Memorial Fellowship in Menton, France. His favourite beach remains Caroline Bay, in Timaru, for its pleasurable associations with his youth.

John MacKinven

John grew up in Titirangi and Takapuna and was educated at Westlake Boys High School and the University of Auckland, where in 2006 he completed a Masters in Creative Writing. His story, 'Hokianga', was part of his university degree submission. John's working life has been spent as a craft artist, teacher and more recently, as a freelance editor and writer. He lives in Auckland with his partner and their two children. Beaches are a recurring presence in his life because they are so compatible with his other interests: travel, walking, drinking and reading. His favourite beaches are Opoutere (wild surf, long walks, the spirit of Michael King), Raumati (sunsets behind the South Island, the lodestone presence of Kapiti Island) and Cheltenham (the Edwardian ambience of old Devonport, plus North Head and Rangitoto).

Linda Niccol

Linda Niccol started life near the beach at Raumati and was educated at Epsom Girls' Grammar School and Wellington Polytechnic. Her first book was a short story collection, *The Geometry of Desire* (2005), and in 2006 she won the prestigious British Short Screenplay Competition. She has recently completed a second collection of short stories, *The Sea Harrow*. Linda lives on the Kapiti Coast, overlooking Raumati, her second favourite beach, which has inspired a number of her short stories. Her favourite beach is Ladies Bay, near Kohimarama.

Carl Nixon

Carl was born and raised in Christchurch, where he still lives, with his wife and their two young children. A novelist, short story writer and playwright, his first book, *Fish 'n' Chip Shop Song and other stories* (Random House New Zealand, 2006) was short-listed for the Commonwealth Writers Prize Best First Book (South-East Asia and the South Pacific). Random House New Zealand also published his novel *Rocking Horse Road* in 2007, the same year that his latest play, *The Raft*, premiered at the Court Theatre in Christchurch and 'My Beautiful Balloon' won the Katherine Mansfield Short Story Award. Sumner beach, close to Cave Rock, is his favourite, 'especially since my wife and I have had kids. It's a great beach for rock climbing, paddling, cave exploration; never exactly the same two days running,' Carl writes.

Maurice Shadbolt

Maurice Shadbolt (1932-2004) was born in Auckland and educated at Te Kuiti High School, Avondale College and the University of Auckland. He was the author of twelve novels, four collections of short stories, two volumes of memoir, a play and several works of non-fiction. 'The Paua Gatherers' is from his first published book, *The New Zealanders* (1959).

Maurice won numerous fellowships and almost every New Zealand literary prize, some of them more than once. In 1989 he was awarded a CBE for services to New Zealand literature. Although he never mentioned a favourite beach, the small, secluded bay below his house in Titirangi appeared in his writing with a frequency that indicated his deep affection for it. Swimming, gathering shellfish and putting a net out there overnight for flounder and other fish were favourite distractions from his writing.

Tina Shaw

Tina was raised on a farm in the Waikato. She went on to attend three universities and have a daughter. A short story writer, novelist and children's writer, she held the Buddle Findlay Sargeson Fellowship in 1999, the Creative New Zealand Berlin Writer's Residency in 2002 and during 2005 was Writer in Residence at the University of Waikato. In the same year her fifth novel, *The Black Madonna* was published. The setting for her story 'Breathless' is her idea of the perfect beach, and although it uses elements from various real ones (the pink shells, for example, come from Omaha), it is otherwise completely fictional. Tina lives in Auckland with her partner and their dog.

Sarah Weir

Sarah was born in Wimbledon, London, and brought up in South Wales. After meeting a group of Kiwis in a squat she decided to visit New Zealand and stayed for twelve years. Although qualified as an agricultural biochemist and a psychotherapist, she also began writing in New Zealand. Her stories have been published in *Takahe*, *Sport* and broadcast on Radio New Zealand. She has won the Joan Faulkner Blake short story competition, was runner-up in the *Takahe* short story award, and her short fiction has been anthologised. Her favourite New Zealand beach is Whangamata, where she has stayed in a friend's bach. Sarah says,

'It has everything: long, wind-swept walks, an island to wade out to and great swimming and boogie boarding'.

Fay Weldon

Fay was conceived in New Zealand, born in England, and then when she was six weeks old, returned to New Zealand. She attended St Margarets, St Marys and Elmwood primary schools, spent one term at Coromandel District primary school, then went to Christchurch Girls' High. In 1946, on her fifteenth birthday, her mother took her back to England. She has degrees in economics and psychology from the University of St Andrews, in Scotland, was awarded the CBE and is a fellow of the Royal Society of Literature. A novelist, screenwriter and journalist, Fay lives on a windswept hill in Dorset with her husband. She has four sons, three stepsons and six grandchildren. Her favourite beach is Piha, on Auckland's west coast. She says, 'It's an archetypal beach – sand, sea, surf – cliffs which are covered with pohutukawas, and a library, and even a dunny'.

Acknowledgements

'A Summer Thing' by Alice Glenday was first published in *A Population of One* (Vintage, 1991); 'Waiariki' by Patricia Grace was first published in *Waiariki and other Stories* (Longman Paul Ltd., 1975); 'Piha Dunny Do' by Fay Weldon first appeared in the UK in *Saga* magazine; 'Kenneth's Friend' by Owen Marshall was first published in *The Day Hemingway Died* (John McIndoe,1984); 'Why I Never learned to Swim' by David Lyndon Brown was first published in *Calling the Fish & Other Stories* (University of Otago Press, 2001); 'Peace In Our Time' by Kevin Ireland first appeared in *Penguin 25 New Fiction* (Penguin Books, 1998); 'Hokianga' by John MacKinven was published in *The Herald on Sunday* in December 2007; 'Summer Love' by Graeme Lay first appeared in *The Town on the Edge of the World* (Tandem Press, 2002); 'Pararaha' by Charlotte Grimshaw also appeared in *The Herald on Sunday* in January 2008; James George's *Hummingbird* was published by Huia Publishers in 2003; 'The Paua Gatherers' by Maurice Shadbolt was first published in *The New Zealanders* (Victor Gollancz, 1959); 'The Rip' by Christine Johnstone was broadcast by Radio New Zealand in 2005; 'Free as a Bird' was published in *Landfall* in 1993; 'My Beautiful Balloon' by Carl Nixon also appeared in the *New Zealand Listener* in January 2008 and in *The Best New Zealand Fiction 5* (edited by Owen Marshall, 2008); 'All the Soul-and-Body Scars' was broadcast by Radio New Zealand in 2002 and appeared in the magazines

Fiddlehead (Canada) in 2001 and *The New Writer* (UK) in 2002 and 'Reading the Waves' by Jackie Davis was published in *Down to the sea again* (HarperCollins, 2005) and was broadcast by Radio New Zealand in 2006. All the other stories in the anthology are published for the first time.

SG8707

Hospital
Goat - Butcher   Hypnotherapy
Psychotherapist   - Past life Regression.
Meditation

        EFT   Emotion Fusion Therapy

        Reshmi   lady   - Sara

Yoga   Body Mind Spirit
                    Spirit - Body Shacra
Shacras   root Shacra

Breathing
Focusing
Allow Flow in body
        Stale energy